Just
North
of
Luck

Susan Whitfield

Cover concept by Susan Whitfield

This is a work of fiction, and is produced from the author's imagination. People, places and things mentioned in this novel are used in a fictional manner.

ISBN 978-0-9960683-1-4 (Trade paperback)
ISBN 978-0-9960683-2-1 (eBook Edition)

Printed in the United States of America
Smashwords Edition, License Notes

Acknowledgements

Tremendous gratitude is due the team of people who made this book possible.

Special thanks to Gladys Prince, who enthusiastically sat beside me for untold hours, honing passages into good prose;

to my pal, Mary Daly, who traveled with me on research and inspirational trips, and for her expertise in technology;

to my daughter-in-law, Kim, for expert guidance on matters of psychology;

to my fantastic family for their inexhaustible love and support;

to friends who have truly overwhelmed me with their loyalty;

and to readers and fans who insist that The Logan Hunter Mystery Series continue.

Just North of Luck is dedicated to the memory of my father, John David Eakins, and to my mother, Neal Graham Eakins, who instilled in me a love of The Blue Ridge Mountains of North Carolina.

1

He hurled his coat into his camo truck and lit a cigarette. Dr. Janah Zack, the Dulcimer High School principal, gave him five minutes to get off the school campus. She'd fired him for peeping at girls in the locker room. He sneered. He'd been doing it for years, those firm asses just begging to be watched. High-school girls had such good-looking hard bodies in little skirts with bright colored thongs showing where their tops didn't meet. They didn't mind advertising their assets. Smart enough not to touch them, he sure did enjoy looking, envying the high school boys who didn't even know how good they had it.

Where he'd made his mistake today was stepping on the tip of that damned broom, sending the handle over to hit the janitor's closet door with a loud bang. The sound spooked the girls, and one darted to the office while two others opened the closet door to reveal him.

I should've run.

But that wasn't his style. He figured he could talk his way out of it, but Dr. Zack didn't buy his story, and the school's deputy detained him while she and the assistant principal went to check the closet—unlocked, a violation of the Madison County Safe Schools Policy. Zack found tiny holes in the door large enough to peek through. They'd been bored with a drill bit, sealing his fate since he always carried his tools, including a drill and bits, in his truck.

He stomped out the cigarette and opened the truck door. John Roman, the head custodian, approached with his self-righteous attitude and puppy-dog eyes.

"I warned you about messing with those girls. Dr. Zack called the superintendent. She wants your school keys." He ignored Roman's outstretched palm and walked around the truck, kicking each tire as though he were checking the air in them, taking his time with the demand. Roman followed.

He stopped and lit another cigarette, blowing smoke in Roman's face before he dropped the keys on the steel ring in the janitor's callused hand and climbed into the truck, not uttering a word. He cranked it and drove off, dropping down the steep drive where the sixteen buses were parked, past the school mascot sign with the stupid-looking moose, and read the words on it as he drove out: *Dulcimer High School of Distinction—Succeeding with the ABCs.* He could come up with his own meaning for the ABCs, he thought with a grin. No one knew about his other set of keys.

Git out from behind that thar chair and git in the bed. It'll all be over in a few minutes and you can cry your pussy face to sleep.

2

A month after his dismissal, the Madison County Public Schools Maintenance Department still hadn't replaced him. He knew that made John Roman's work day more demanding, and probably longer. Roman wasn't a skilled carpenter, and he wasn't a certified electrician either, so the school would have to call the central office and wait for repairs and new work orders. He figured he'd saved them large amounts of money over the years because he could paint, caulk, install, or repair light fixtures, and even repair drywall. Roman couldn't even paint worth a damn.

He'd quickly tired of Roman's constant preaching about his peeping at girls and the sexual comments he made to some of the young, good-looking teachers. Roman warned he could be fired for sexual harassment if he were caught, but the way he figured it, the teachers enjoyed it and considered it a compliment from a handsome man. None of them complained.

Now he'd been caught. He wondered if Roman's freaking blabbermouth had anything to do with it. He already knew the janitor kissed butt, always willing to lick Dr. Zack's ass. He'd eat steamy shit for that woman. But he did sympathize a little with Roman having to go home every day and work just as hard—cooking, cleaning, and taking care of a sick wife.

He glanced at his glowing watch face when he heard the truck coming around the school building. Six o'clock. He'd parked so his pickup hid from Roman's headlights, easy enough to do with the school sitting atop a mountain. He knew the janitor's routine of picking up trash on campus after students left and throwing the bags in the bed of his truck until the next morning. He drew in a breath of crisp air as the truck approached the Dumpster.

He watched the janitor hop out of his truck, gather his brown corduroy coat around him, and reach for two trash bags. At that moment Roman's eyes focused on him. Maybe the lit cigarette gave him away.

"Who's there?" John called out, taken off guard. The cigarette went to the ground without response. He saw Roman reach in the truck, and as he turned with his flashlight, the 2x4 slammed into his head.

Throwing a large thick sheet of plastic over the janitor as he lay on the ground, he spun the diminutive man until the plastic ran out. He walked to his truck and got his wide duct tape, wrapping it tightly, turning Roman into a plastic mummy. He took his victim's flashlight and checked the breath vapor inside the plastic. A crooked smirk inched across his face.

He picked up Roman and deposited him upside down in the large, heavy-duty steel trashcan before grabbing his cigarette butt and the 2x4. He got into his truck, keeping his gloves on until he could throw the board over the mountain into some thick kudzu vines on his way to have some breakfast at Pappy's.

•

I'll find you, you bastard! You better git to this house right now, boy! I ain't playin'! It'll be worse if you don't come on heah.

•

After finishing off a plate of hotcakes and sausage, he left the money on the table and climbed into his truck. He put Roman's flashlight under the seat after rubbing prints off and adding a few of his own. It was time to fix old Mr. Chester's porch with the new screen in the truck bed. He could tear out the old rotten screen and replace it by dinnertime and head for the Mars Hill College Library to begin building computer pods for the new on-line classes they'd offer in the summer.

~~~~~

He passed the school on his way back from breakfast and decided to pull into the woods across from the school and let his truck disappear into its surroundings. He held his saw in his hand in case someone spotted him and asked questions, he could say he planned to cut a few pieces of firewood. He watched with high-powered binoculars as Janah Zack pulled her Sequoia up the steep hill and into her parking space, running a comb through her black hair, a gene from her Cherokee mother, then flossing the gap in her front teeth, a gene from her black father.

He noticed two hysterical maids running around the building, flailing their arms and pointing to the back of the school. Dr. Zack's tires squealed as she sped around the building, no doubt to where Roman's truck more than likely still idled. Another SUV turned in and the maids waved it around back.

After a few minutes, wailing sirens came up the mountain. Madison County Sheriff's cars screeched into the drive and barreled up the hill and around back, one driven by the detective, What's-His-Name. He sat there a few more minutes before easing his truck onto the road and whistling his way toward the northwest.

3

I couldn't avoid hitting the suicidal skunk as it scampered into my path on the curvy six-lane section of Interstate 40, one side of the highway mountain rock, the other, abyss. I squashed it with my Hummer, spewing fluids up the side windows while I gasped and grabbed my nose hard enough to knock my wire-framed glasses cockeyed.

"Arrgh!" I swerved at the breathtaking odor. A horn protested beside me as I slowed and yanked the tank into the slow lane so I could exit at the first opportunity, probably many miles ahead. If the impact propelled body parts underneath, I might have to ride all the way to the Asheville city limits with the stink making me nauseous.

The SBI assigned me to Madison County, known as the Gem of the Blue Ridge because of its breathtaking views and high peaks. My first assignment as a full-fledged agent: to expose a major moonshine operation hidden in its jagged terrain. I, Agent Logan Hunter, a single white female from Genesis Beach, inexperienced in bootlegging operations and mountains, was instructed to relocate somewhere between Asheville and the Tennessee line.

Finding my own place to live in this remote area became part of my initiation into the agency. And I could complain about not being immediately assigned to a major case like murder, but to get any assignment that kept me away from a desk so recently after being sworn in made me happy. I'd been given a homicide kit to keep in the Hummer at all times—just in case. It included a journal for documentation, plastic and paper evidence bags, crime tape, various sizes of tweezers, a pack of Sharpies to label evidence, paper booties, and a box of thick gloves, some with metal tips. I should be ready for anything.

~~~~~

I found a car wash and gave the Hummer the ten-dollar royal treatment, under carriage and all. I spent my first night downtown at the Renaissance Asheville to gather some information before deciding on a place to stay. Besides, the forecast called for snow showers. I wondered if I'd need thermal long johns or a set of Cuddle Duds.

That's something I didn't think about.

I didn't know how long this assignment would be, since moonshine operations were on going and the mountain terrain thick and treacherous.

I'd worked out on rock-climbing equipment to prepare for this assignment, not sure that prepared me enough. Altitude and other obstacles needed to be factored in. My uniform was camouflage, right down to the boots, but at least I could choose my own underwear.

I had authority to call for the SBI's Special Response Team, or SRT, once I located an illegal still. The SRT is a twenty-seven-member unit that assists with high-risk and hostage situations and helps plan strategic raids. Other agents would be on call with a Cessna and helicopter if needed. Boats were on standby in case bootleggers tried to flee down the French Broad River.

My room on the tenth floor offered huge windows, framing a picturesque Blue Ridge Mountain range. I drank it in. The mountains always gave me a sense of peace, no matter what else was going on in my life. I unpacked the small duffel I brought up, checked my newly issued Ruger M2014 with laser sight, and showered.

After enjoying fried green tomatoes with corn sauce in the hotel restaurant, I pulled out my maps to study, gave my glasses a wipe with the curtain lining, and sat in a chair facing the panoramic scene until I began to yawn. I hopped into bed, switching on the television and getting the weather forecast: two to four inches of early spring white powder for the central mountains.

~~~~~

Asheville transformed into a glass wonderland. Snow, sealed by sleet, blanketed the earth as far as I could see. The air promised more bad weather. I could no longer see the mountains in the distance, the only movement gentle swaying of glass limbs and a few frantic birds dodging in and out of shelter.

I did some aerobics and donned my boots, layering a couple of shirts under a hooded sweatshirt before jogging for eight blocks near the hotel, careful of my footing. The cold March air stung my lungs but it felt good. Clear, pristine air always gave me a high I kept long after my morning shower.

I got the call as I packed to leave the hotel and head toward Hot Springs, where I hoped to find something affordable to rent while I worked the high mountain ranges.

"Hunter?" I recognized Kent Poletti, my direct supervisor. "Where are you?"

"In a hotel in Asheville, sir."

"Good. Turn on your television and get the scoop on the murder of a custodian at a high school not too far from you. Even though the Madison County Sheriff's Department is on the scene, I want you to stop by and see if they need any help."

"But sir, isn't it their call?"

"Sure is, but since you're around, just take a look. Murder is rare in that area. But Logan," his voice softened, "don't interfere. We don't want any trouble. Just stop by and then take off."

"So you don't want me to badge my way in?"

"Definitely not." *Good.* I told him I'd be back in touch.

I flipped on the TV, surfed to the local news channel, and saw the scene at Dulcimer High School. A huge man, who resembled an overweight bulldog, introduced himself as Sheriff Amos Yandle.

"The body of head custodian John Roman was found about seven o'clock this morning when two maids reported to work. They saw his truck and went to find out why he hadn't disabled the school alarms like he did every school day. They saw feet wrapped in plastic, screamed, and ran around the building just as Dr. Janah Zack, the school's principal, drove into her parking space. They were both hysterical.

"Dr. Zack dialed 9-1-1 as she drove around the school's campus to the back of the gym. Evan Lovingood, the new varsity basketball coach at Dulcimer High School, pulled up beside her. Together they found Mr. Roman's body wrapped in layers of thick plastic. His truck was nearby, still running," the sheriff reported. He said the family had been notified, and promised to assign all available manpower to the case.

The massive sheriff stepped aside and a lady with coal-black hair came to the microphone. She wore a light blue tweed suit and a shaken expression.

"I'm Janah Zack, principal of Dulcimer High School. John Roman was a good man, hardworking, dependable, and loyal. The faculty, staff, and students loved him. This is a sad day for us. Our hearts go out to his wife, Pat. Please keep all of us in your prayers. Thank you." She disappeared inside the building on the arm of a good-looking black man.

4

"Excuse me, sir?" I pulled the emergency brake beside the silver and royal Madison County Sheriff's car. A blond, wavy-haired officer who was writing in a journal turned and eyeballed my Hummer and me. A smile broke out across his gorgeous face.

"Let me guess," the hunk said. "With this ride you have to be reinforcement of some kind." He smashed his hands into the pockets of his black windbreaker with the Madison County Detective badge pinned to the front.

"My name's Logan Hunter." I pulled out my SBI badge.

"You're quick. I didn't even know we'd called you guys…uh, gals," the hunk responded, giving my hand a firm shake.

"I was already in the area and heard about the incident and just dropped by. I'm not here to get in the way, Detective. I'm just offering assistance if needed and wanted," I explained, not wanting to ruffle any feathers. Poletti had reminded me that some local law enforcement officers resent SBI agents taking over cases in their territories. I had no interest in making enemies this early in my career.

"Chase Railey, detective for Madison County Sheriff's Department. So, what's your assignment?"

"Bootleggers."

We both laughed.

"I wish you were with us. I could use some help. Our department's small. I'm the only investigator and my background is limited, especially with murder. The sheriff and grounds crew have left. So has the body. I'm still trying to document everything we know so far. You have experience with murder?"

"Yeah, some."

"If you've got a few minutes, could you go with me to question the principal? Maybe you'd put her at ease, and keep me straight too." His eyes weren't blue; they were tanzanite and they yanked me in like a shop vac sucking water.

"I can't do that. This isn't my jurisdiction."

"I'm not asking you to take over, but it would be nice to have another set of eyes and ears."

"Sorry."

"Well," he stretched out his hand, "it was nice meeting you."

Crap! Couldn't he try a little harder?

I wrestled with the idea of helping Chase Railey while he stood near the Hummer door.

"Nice to meet you as well." He started to walk off. "Are you going to give up so easily?" He turned and smiled.

"Does that mean you'll help me?"

"If you're sure I won't interfere. I don't want your sheriff filing a complaint against me."

"It's my idea. Don't worry about it." He grinned. We walked to the scene of the crime but stayed outside the tape. I felt awkward enough without stepping on someone else's evidence.

"Two maids found the victim, John Roman. They ran to get the principal, Dr. Zack, when she got here. They were hysterical so somebody took them home. Right after Dr. Zack arrived, Coach Lovingood got here," he stated, checking his pocket notepad. "Coach pulled John Roman from the school's trash can. He was wrapped in thick plastic. Apparent suffocation. Gruesome. Moisture in the bag means he was still alive when he was wrapped in it, and it looked like he tried to claw his way out of the plastic." Railey's eyes lifted to meet mine. "His fingertips were bloody and the plastic was full of bloody scratches. Nobody should die like that."

I nodded and adjusted my specs.

"Dr. Zack called 9-1-1 and the superintendent to initiate the school's crisis plan, which worked well. A trooper stationed at the entrance sent all cars and their passengers away. He's still there, I think."

"He is. I had to show him my badge to get in," I said.

"All school personnel were told to report to the National Guard Armory. I think they bussed folks on home from there if they needed transportation. None of them will be allowed back on school grounds today." Railey closed his notepad. "Dr. Zack and the coach were just staring at the plastic when I got here and cut it away."

"Did you take pictures?"

"Yeah, we have a deputy who did. Some of them will be tough to look at," he said holding the school door for me. "I told the coach to take the principal inside. He's staying to screen calls and keep folks away from her. Except me, of course." He looked at me and beamed. *Of course.*

We walked into the main office and the tall, handsome black man I'd seen on television stood to greet us. His shaved head reached skyward, so I figured he was the basketball coach, and about my age with an athletic build. I imagined aggressive high school girls were his biggest challenge.

"Coach Lovingood, this is Agent Hunter. SBI," Chase Railey announced. "We need to talk to Dr. Zack if she's up to it."

The shaved head towered over us. He verged on seven feet. His dark arm crossed in front of us. "Nobody's bothering her. She needs this time alone. Come back later."

"Sir, we understand she's upset. We just have a few questions and we'll go, for the time being."

"I told you—" The door squeaked open and the tiny lady I'd seen on TV appeared, with disheveled hair.

"Coach, thank you for screening, but I need to talk with these people."

"Yes, ma'am. If you're sure. I'll be right here all day long. Let me know if you need anything."

"How about some coffee?" she asked us. We nodded. "Coach, can you make a pot for us?"

"Yes, ma'am."

"Come in, Detective. You'll have to pardon Coach Lovingood. He's trying to protect me. And pardon my appearance. I tend to run my fingers through my hair when I'm distressed." She patted her hair down with one hand and, with the other, motioned us to chairs in front of her desk. She glanced at me. "I'm Janah Zack."

"Logan Hunter, ma'am. SBI. This is Detective Railey's investigation. I'm just passing by."

"Then why—"

"I asked her for her opinion, Dr. Zack," Railey interjected. I squirmed.

Janah Zack straightened her suit jacket over her potbelly.

"I love this school. I've been here four years. Prior to administration, I taught English for ten years. I've never implemented a crisis plan until today." She wrung her hands and shook her head, looking down at her desk.

Chase Railey began his questions. "Dr. Zack, are you aware of any enemies Mr. Roman might have?"

"No, Detective Railey. As far as I know everyone liked him. He did many thoughtful things for teachers and students. And especially for me. He could make the best apple turnovers you ever put in your mouth," she said, glancing around her office. "He was sixty just two weeks ago, and the Hospitality Committee gave a cake and ice cream social for him right after school. It touched him. We all realized what a hard life he had."

"What do you mean?"

"He worked at the textile mill over near Mars Hill until it closed. He needed to work so he could have state benefits. You know, hospitalization insurance. I was glad to get him. Such a hard worker. His wife has lupus. It's robbed her of all her strength and vitality. She's such a sweet lady, too. John said she never complains. The medical bills have been a constant burden, but the state benefits helped some. I don't know what will become of her now."

~~~~~

Evan Lovingood appeared at the door with a coffee pot and three Styrofoam cups. He glanced at us with an apology. "Dr. Zack, one of the teachers is on the phone. She says she needs to report something that might be important about John. Do you want to talk to her?"

"Who is it?" The principal seemed in a daze.

"It's Ella Goforth. She said something happened at the baseball game Friday night."

Dr. Zack picked up the phone and put it on *Speaker*. Chase Railey and I leaned forward to listen in.

"Ella?"

"Dr. Zack, I just can't believe such a thing could happen. I remember noticing a problem at the baseball game Friday night, though. Mr. Roman had words with some students. I don't know what about, but he made them mad, and they were calling him names and giving him the finger as they walked away. Did he report it to you?"

"No, no, he didn't say a word about it. Do you know who the students were?"

Ella had no idea. Janah Zack thanked her for the information and hung up.

"A ruckus at the game Friday night? My assistant principal worked that game. He never mentioned a problem, but maybe he'll know who they were."

"Dr. Zack, we'll need to talk with the assistant principal. This may get more difficult for you and the school if students were involved."

"His name is Tucker Klixx. He's in charge of the crisis plan, but he should be about through with that. I'll call him to come over." Chase wrote the name on his pad.

The coach appeared in the doorway again. "Dr. Zack, detectives, it just occurred to me we have surveillance cameras. Do you think they might have caught something?"

The principal jumped out of her chair and ran around the desk with her office keys. "My God, Evan! I didn't think about that." She turned to us and explained, "They're so new. They were just installed several weeks ago." She unlocked the assistant principal's office door and we followed her to the computer monitor. She ran the videotape back on the camera nearest the Dumpster to 5:45 that morning and we glued our eyes to the monitor.

"The problem might be that up on this mountain, the cameras can't possibly pick up activities in the periphery," the principal said.

We could only make out an outlying yard light and some early morning fog on the camera. When the video reached 5:54 we saw a distant pair of headlights, but there wasn't enough daylight to make out whether it was a car, truck, bus, or ATV. The lights disappeared off the side of the camera span. At 6:06 another set of headlights appeared much closer to the crime scene. John Roman's truck, we surmised. It was still too dark to see anyone, or exactly what happened.

"Somebody was lying in wait. It's a damn shame it was so dark," Railey said.

"John has the only keys to the gate except for me. I don't know how anyone else got in unless they were on a motorcycle or four-wheel," Janah said softly, still watching the screen.

"Do you have students or teachers who ride motorcycles to school?" Chase asked. She shook her head.

"The headlights are too far apart to be a four-wheel and it's certainly not a motorcycle light," I added.

"Dr. Zack, didn't Mrs. Goforth tell you about some trouble at the game? Will the video tape go back that far?" the coach asked.

"It should." She backed up the video to Friday night's game and located the camera covering the baseball field, down the mountain from the rest of the campus. No camera reached as far over as the trash cans and even though we watched for about forty-five minutes, we found nothing. We scrutinized the film while Dr. Zack made the call to the assistant principal, ten minutes away.

Detective Railey told Dr. Zack and Coach Lovingood he'd be back to question some students and he wanted copies of the video from Friday until this morning. He opened the door, letting me walk out first.

"I need some fresh air. How about you?"

"This is certainly fresh," I said, shoving my hands deep into my pockets and breathing in the air's crispness.

He smiled, and even though I looked down and away, I knew his eyes scoped my long body. We walked down the hill to the trooper and Chase instructed him to let Mr. Klixx in when he arrived.

We stood around outside, checking out the school yard and each other until we saw a light blue Taurus turn in the drive, wave at the trooper, and park in the AP parking space. Janah Zack waited near the front lobby to speak to Klixx when he entered. They hugged and went back into her office. We followed close behind.

"Detective Railey, Agent Hunter, this is Tucker Klixx, the assistant principal," Janah Zack said. Klixx dragged a chair from the reception area and sat beside me.

"It's awful. I can't imagine why this happened. John Roman was a decent man."

Dr. Zack reached over and touched his arm. "Tucker, Ella Goforth called and gave details about a confrontation between John and some students at the game Friday night. Do you know anything about that?"

"I remember seeing John talking to some kids near the trash cans, but it certainly didn't seem confrontational. John came over and stood by me at the left field fence after that and never mentioned it."

Railey sat up straighter. "Mr. Klixx, can you identify the students?"

"Yeah, let me think a minute. I can ID several of them. Um, Tait Glott and his shadow, what's his face. Uh," he rubbed the sides of his forehead, "Scott Raindance. Tait can't breathe without Raindance. And two girls, freshmen, I think. Meg and Ashland."

"Do you know last names?"

"Margaret Lucas. Everybody calls her Meg. And Ashland Lawrence. The four were walking around together. You know, like freshmen do, flirting and giggling. I think those four I saw near John, but, like I said, he never told me about any trouble. And he didn't appear to be upset when he stood with me."

Railey turned to the principal. "We'd like to question those students, Dr. Zack."

I cleared my throat. "He means *he'd* like to question them. I'm not on this case and I've overstayed. Please excuse me." I stood, feeling awkward I'd allowed myself to stay so long, caught up in the excitement. I shook hands with the administrators, and looking at Chase Railey, wished them luck with the investigation.

The detective knitted his brow. "I'll walk you out." When we reached the Hummer he said, "Thanks for coming in with me."

"No problem."

"If you plan to find the stills, I hope you're a good hiker and have tough skin."

"I prepared by climbing some rock walls."

"Were any of them covered with thick kudzu vines? You can strangle yourself and lose half your weapons and gear in that mess," he pointed out.

I'd noticed the thick vines and how prolific they were. Even the telephone poles were covered and unrecognizable from the growth, spiraling from dead winter brown to spring green at an alarming rate.

"Detective, it was nice to meet you," I said as I climbed into the Hummer.

Chase Railey walked over to my door and peeked inside.

"By the way," I leaned out. "Any ideas on where the stills are?"

Railey pointed in three different directions twisting a

little as he spoke. "That way. Over there. And over that way."

We both laughed.

"If I go to work for the SBI, can I have one of these?"

I closed the door and cranked up, still smiling at him. I couldn't help it. He was mesmerizing.

"Nope."

I drove down the school drive, leaving him standing in the mountain mist with a quizzical look on his face. While I didn't mind my moonshine assignment, I found murder much more intriguing, not to mention Chase Railey, who wasn't wearing a wedding band. But really, why did I care?

5

I went up the mountain on Route 63, looking for Luck and Trust. I figured I'd find solitude up toward Hot Springs and be near the assignment as well. I hadn't made a reservation to stay at The Hot Springs Hotel, The Mountain Magnolia Inn, or anywhere else for that matter, but I hoped I wouldn't have to drive all the way back to Asheville. The narrow roads rose into white clouds, looking like they'd been combed from knots to tangles to waves to wispy strands. I reduced my speed as the curves became more severe and the guardrails disappeared. No more watching the clouds. I gulped, hoping I didn't meet any traffic from the other direction on these switchbacks. It reminded me of a phrase my daddy always used in the mountains, "You meet yourself coming back."

I came to the intersection of Route 63 and Highway 209. I saw the Trust General Store and Grill a few yards away, pulled over, and went inside. The man behind the counter said Luck was just a sign and a church, just south of Trust. Neither were towns, just dots on a map, he said. I asked about places to stay or to rent and he said I'd better go to Hot Springs. I picked up a tiny jar of tomato jam, curiosity influencing me to buy it. I stepped toward the door as a blonde middle-aged woman made a noisy entrance.

"I couldn't help but notice your Hummer and overhear your question. I'm Taryn Kosterman. I have a house just a couple of miles from here." She threw out her large heavily bejeweled hand and I shook it.

"I'm Logan Hunter. No hotels, huh?"

They both shook their heads.

"There's a couple of hotels in Hot Springs, but they stay booked up by tourists. You'd have to make a reservation months ahead to stay there," the blonde explained.

"Thanks for the information anyway. I guess it's back to Asheville."

"Weaverville is closer," the man said.

"I remember coming through there. That'll be fine. Not quite so far back."

~~~~~

I drove to a white church less than a mile away. I pulled into the lopsided grass yard and paused to look at the pristine white steeple. I loved old white churches nestled in mountain valleys. Three dogwood trees were alive with blooms, like suspended snowflakes, each one unique. I was glad the ice and snow missed this area and hadn't damaged them.

I heard a toot and glanced around to see the blonde in her dark blue Pathfinder. Taryn Kosterman waved.

"Listen, like I said, I have this huge house, and live alone since my husband died. Are you looking for something temporary, or a rental?"

"I need a temporary rental, I suppose," I responded. She looked puzzled. "I'm an SBI agent, assigned to a case here. I don't know how long it'll take."

"You're welcome to stay with me. I teach, but I'm home most nights. My house is big and you could have your privacy. Your own bedroom and bath, already furnished. You could even have your own private entrance," Taryn offered.

It sounded more interesting than driving back to Asheville or Weaverville.

"You can follow me if you want. I'm fixin' to go home now," she grinned, driving off before I responded. I decided to take a look since it was late in the day, but I wasn't interested in being a lonesome widow's entertainment every night, so I'd keep my options open.

I followed the SUV down Route 209 south to a dirt and gravel drive. It started to rain, but I could see the top of a sprawling white board frame house with a red roof and trim. The vivacious blonde bounded out of her vehicle, agile as she started up the slanted yard ahead of me carrying a cooler. Her shoulder-length straight platinum hair with bangs matched her personality. I watched my footing to catch up with her once I closed the Hummer door.

Taryn Kosterman talked nonstop as we approached the front of the house, where a laid stone path divided a yard filled with early spring flowers and bushes, giving way to the lush forest beyond. We walked up the short path to the red porch and Taryn opened the front door. I hesitated in order to take a good look at the house. It had many different roof pitches, all framed in red. A huge window stood out directly over the front porch. I twisted to view the forest and seasonal flowering plants with great pleasure, and then walked inside.

Taryn put her mail on a nearby table. I could tell I'd like the warmth and color of this house. I walked around in the den, trying to take in the many artistic details, all hitting my eyes at once. She watched my reaction.

"Wow!" I exclaimed. "This is great! I love it!"

"I'm an artist as well as an art teacher. Most of these things I made myself. My husband always thought I overdid a bit, but he endured it, bless his soul," Taryn said. "I made these little footstools and the gold mirror over the fireplace." Taryn pointed to a crewel-embroidered footstool and moved another with a leopard skin top so I wouldn't have to sidestep it. Both stools had legs made from animal horns.

Mrs. Kosterman walked over to the mantle, straightening her hair in a small mirror framed by what I assumed was her own interpretation of the sun. It filled the entire brickwork.

"Set a spell, Agent Hunter," she said, motioning me to a nearby rattan chair with a pink print pillow. "I'll start a load of laundry and put on some stew and a mess of greens I just bought, and then I'll show you the rest of the house. You'll stay for supper, won't you?"

"I don't want to impose, but it certainly sounds good." I sat in the chair and glanced over at the dark wood bench in front of the window. A vase of flowers I recognized from the yard, several art books, and one partly melted candle sat on it. A pile of books nested near my foot, on top of which sat an opened magazine and an empty cup and saucer.

"Did you paint the fire screen?" I called out just as Taryn appeared in the doorway.

"No, my grandmother's screen. I think it adds a little more nostalgia to this room. I hang out here when I'm not in the kitchen or up in my studio." Taryn reached for the cup and saucer and walked toward the kitchen. I stood and followed her. My eyes went to the high wood ceiling and I didn't know what to focus on next. Taryn grinned at me and laughed.

"I figure I live up this dirt path in the most beautiful place on Earth and I want all the things I love around me," Taryn explained as she lifted a copper colander from the huge metal pot rack over the island. The old porcelain sink—probably part of the original house—looked a little small for the massive window behind it. I walked over to the pale yellow and green stove from generations ago.

"My grandmother's," Taryn pointed out. "Still works too. It's gas, so if I lose power—which happens frequently in the winter—I can still cook." I walked over to the breakfast nook.

"I took down some of the old fence around the place and hired a local carpenter to make this corner piece of fence into a breakfast nook for eating or reading. You'll notice I have reading spots throughout the house."

"I love books, too."

A closed porch converted into an informal dining room with ladder-back chairs and more glorious windows, some etched. Above the oak table, a star light reminded me of the ones used at Christmas, but this one was permanently attached and looked great.

I wasn't accustomed to so many stimuli. I'd grown up at the beach, with no rugs or carpet, and few knickknacks other than seashells collected for years and piled in bowls for open displays.

A skinny well-scrubbed table stood between the cabinets and me. I walked over to the tall decorative container on it. It contained at least ten pounds of rice.

"Oh." Taryn giggled. "That's supposed to be a driveway lantern top, but when the wiring stopped working, I cut the wires off and brought it inside to make good use of it." Her artistic genius intrigued me. Taryn motioned me to a cozy chair with a rooster pillow and she pulled the rattan chair closer to me.

I heard a noise like the slamming and banging of a garbage truck. Taryn jumped, and I followed her cursing to the laundry room.

"This damned washer is fixin' to go. I've had it. It'll be my next purchase," she said, apologizing for her cursing. We headed to the porch after she dialed the stew to a higher setting.

"So you're an SBI agent. You're here because of poor Mr. Roman? I just can't believe anybody would kill him, or anyone else for that matter. We've never had this sort of trouble. The folks around here are devoted to each other."

"Yes, I'm an agent, but not sent here for Mr. Roman. I'm working moonshine. The SBI assigned me to this area before this happened. I'm not even involved in that case. Right now the locals are handling it."

"I see."

"So you think the killer's an outsider?"

"I guess. Nobody 'round here would do such a thing. I wish you were involved though. Our law enforcement isn't bad, but they don't have much experience with this sort of thing."

"Did you know Mr. Roman?"

"I knew of him. Quiet, I'm told. He worked at the textile mill, and when it closed, he got the job at Dulcimer High School. His wife is sick and I think he doted on her. I don't know why anyone would kill him. That poor woman is in a mess now," Taryn finished, shaking her blond hair. She started toward the door and turned back.

"Moonshine, huh?"

I nodded, noticing that the rain, now heavier, sounded divine on her tin roof.

"Do you want to see the rest of the house?" Taryn offered. I nodded with anticipation. We walked down a short hall, and when Taryn stopped, I looked around her into a warm inviting bedroom. A quilt in dark rich reds, greens, and golds covered the bed, above the headboard a red berry wreath. This room wasn't as overflowing with visuals as the den.

"This is my bedroom. I love it," she said.

So did I.

I followed her into the adjoining bathroom. The flooring looked like red brick. The fixtures were white porcelain but the sink caught my eye since it set in a thick piece of wood, attached to two ornate metal braces. It was unusual and I liked it almost as much as I liked the shower door.

"This shower door was once a church window, believe it or not. It's copper, so it never mildews. Since the stained glass is a copper color too, I wanted to keep the rest of this room light. Haze DeBrew, the carpenter who made the breakfast nook, put a recessed light in the shower for me."

Mr. DeBrew must be talented.

She opened a bedroom door and we both stepped inside. This room differed from hers, with blue walls, a colorfully stenciled floor, lace curtains, and two matching print overstuffed chairs, the colors pulled from the stencils. The headboard and nightstand were white. An old oil lamp made into an electric lamp, wore a stenciled shade. Yellow roses pulled color from the tiny print in the chairs.

"This would be your room, if you're interested. Not so much clutter. I use it for guests, but I seldom have any. You could fix it anyway you want. I wouldn't mind, except the floor. That took a lot of time and nearly wore off my knee caps," Taryn said as she opened the adjoining door to the white bathroom. "I sometimes call this my summer suite." The towels were happy yellow and ocean blue, folded neatly, on a pedestal table near the tub. I studied the suite for a second, deciding it would more than meet my needs if I accepted. It gave me a sense of peace and tranquility.

"I guess I should ask about using the kitchen and how much you'll charge."

Taryn scratched her blonde coif for a second. "Well, I've never rented a room before. I guess the house is already mine and I have to keep it up whether I rent anything or not. How does $100 a month sound? It's enough to cover your food and electricity. You don't look like you eat much. You just need to let me know if you make long-distance calls on my phone." She waited for my response.

"Are you sure that's enough? I don't mind paying more. And I have my own cell phone so there's no need for me to use your phone at all."

"You'll find your cell won't work in some places in the mountains. And remember, you're not renting a house; you're renting a room. But maybe we can eat together sometimes, and you have the run of the house except for my bedroom and bathroom."

Taryn took me by the arm and led me to the screened-in porch I'd noticed from the breakfast nook. An old brown vinyl chair and an upholstered chair were nestled into a corner with a lamp. A worn round table held a flowering plant and a candle. Several green plants rounded out the cozy spot for reading, writing, or painting, if the weather cooperated. I walked on over to the screened door and gasped. The backyard looked like a painting straight off an artist's easel.

"Breathtaking, isn't it?" A mulch path took my eye to a cedar arbor, created, no doubt, by Taryn. Two heavy metal gates welded together into a point above the cedar. On both sides of this arbor lush green vines, threaded with red berries, ran up the metal. The mulch path, bordered on both sides by an array of purple butterfly bushes and Queen Anne's Lace, went on beyond this arbor where another joined it and appeared to be a path to the woods just a little farther out.

"I spend a lot of time back here, as you might imagine," Taryn explained with pride. We walked back into the kitchen, and she tapped my shoulder and put her finger to her lips to keep me quiet. We peeked back out onto the porch and watched as a raccoon skillfully opened the screen door, went directly to the cooler Taryn had left, opened it, and grabbed an entire package of sausage. The furry bandit gave us a quick grin of satisfaction and scampered out the door.

I must have looked puzzled. "I always get an extra one for Gizmo," she said, taking the rest of her refrigerated groceries inside. She set down the cooler and turned toward a narrow staircase. Without a word she climbed the stairs and I followed. She stepped aside once I reached the top, and I was in her studio.

The palatial window I'd noticed directly above the front porch framed a green pasture surrounded by mountainside. She had an easel here, along with storage cubicles for all sorts of paints, brushes, and projects. A sewing machine and cubicles loaded with fabrics in many colors and textures filled it.

The vaulted ceiling didn't provide good lighting, so she had a high-powered lamp on the oak table she could bend to suit her needs. The largest, most gorgeous dream catcher I'd ever seen suspended from a ceiling beam. I pointed to it and Taryn explained she used a wood quilt frame to create the Mandela dream catcher in combinations of rich reds and teals with many shades of white. The yarns were woven and delicately raked to resemble feathers.

I moved around the enormous room, fascinated by oil paintings, stained glass in many sizes and shapes, quilts in glorious rich hues, piles of grape vine, no doubt for wreath-making, and stopped in front of rusty tin. "What're you going to do with this stuff?"

"I'm making weathervanes for the annual High Country Arts and Crafts Show. Most of this will go." She walked over to a bookcase and opened a drawer, revealing sterling silver jewelry.

"You're magnificent! You should open your own business. Everything is breathtaking. When do you find the time to do all this?"

"When you live alone, the days and nights get pretty long. I'm not much of a sleeper and I'm passionate about my art. Many times I work through the night, especially on the weekends. I'll try to do things at night that won't disturb you, I mean, if you decide to stay."

"How can I resist such a wonderful place? You should rent it, or make an inn."

"No, I'm too persnickety about living with other people. I have a good feeling about you, though. The SBI wouldn't have you if you weren't nice, now would they?" Taryn headed down the stairs.

"I'll take care of my space, and I'm private, so I won't interfere with your lifestyle. I give you my word."

"You're moving in?"

"Yep." I grinned as she gave me an unexpected bear hug. Once we got to the kitchen, Taryn asked me to write a list of foods I like and dislike. She said she'd cook most nights, but when I wouldn't be home to let her know ahead of time, if I could, and she'd do the same. We made a pact to share cooking and cleaning chores and she showed me an entrance near my bedroom I could use if I preferred.

"Feel free to have friends over. You can use any room you wish. I do sometimes watch a movie, but most nights I read or paint," she said, coming out the door with an umbrella to help me get my things from the Hummer.

My first night began well. After a good workout with my MP3, and a warm bath, I piled into the bed to make a few calls before extinguishing the light, so peaceful I knew I'd sleep well even though I was in a strange place.

~~~~~

I couldn't identify the strange noise that woke me sometime during the night. Whooping and hollering. I bolted up and ran to the window overlooking the backyard. I snatched my glasses off the nightstand to make certain I saw what I thought I saw. A naked person ran through the yard. A woman. Boobs bouncing up and around like Bumper Cars at the county fair. Taryn? Naked? I rubbed my eyes and peered again. Yep, Taryn. Stark white naked. But what the hell was she doing?

I knelt beside the windowsill and watched the nude blonde running around in the cool night air, apparently enjoying her romp immensely.

Have I moved in with a woman whose paint pallet is half empty?

I couldn't tear my eyes away from this sight although I knew I should. She eventually wound down and picked up her white gown and panties on the way back toward the porch. I hoped she couldn't see me since I'd left the light off on purpose. I heard her when she came in the house and gave her a minute before walking out like I was looking a late-night snack. I feigned a yawn as I walked into the kitchen.

"Oh, my God, Logan! I completely forgot you were here. Did I wake you?" Thankfully her gown now covered her sizable body.

I tried to act innocent. "Wh…what, I just wanted some milk. What're you doing up?"

"Damned hot flashes. I, uh, sometimes just run outside and peel off my clothes. There's nobody around to see. It's so liberating! And the air feels wonderful after a rain. But I totally forgot you were here. I apologize. Did I scare you?"

"No, I don't know what you're talking about," I lied.

She nodded, and said good night.

6

Sunrise tooted, tweeted, and chirped me awake. I'd rested well and awoke refreshed and eager to run a few miles through Taryn's valley before driving into the Smokies to locate a still. Taryn had left me a couple of bagels and some cream cheese along with fresh coffee and a Thermos for the road. I ate one bagel, stuck the other in a plastic bag, and filled the Thermos. I smiled. I liked Taryn. Hopefully she had good sense. Her stripping in the backyard did bother me a bit. Otherwise, so far so good.

Dressed in rough-terrain camo over lacy underwear, I made sure my emergency blanket and camo pup tent were in the back of the Hummer just in case the weather did a three-sixty. The mountains could produce gales much like the ocean's nor'easters and I needed to take along some water and extra food in case I had to stay out over night. I scrawled Taryn a note not to worry if I didn't come home for a few days. An agent never knew where she'd end up. I dialed Kent Poletti to let him know I was officially starting the investigation and I'd keep in touch.

I drove northwest up the narrow road, continuing on where the centerlines had long ago disappeared. I took my time since guardrails at this altitude were rusted or completely disintegrated. I'd already made one mistake: I wasn't going to find any kind of store to buy water or food.

Several miles later, I spotted smoke just over the next ridge and pulled over at the closest overlook. I fished my Bushnell binoculars from under the seat and got out. Inhaling the mountain air stirred peace through my limbs to my soul. The scenery was breathtaking—at least twenty different shades of blue, mingled with a hint of green. I loved the dark shadows clouds created when they passed between the sun and the mountains. I stood in awe of the Blue Ridge Mountains until a gust of wind brought me back to consciousness.

I scoped the next mountain with the binoculars, zeroing in on a tall stream of smoke deep in the underbrush. I took mental notes, trying to decide its distance from me and if it was simply an Appalachian cabin chimney.

I tried to keep one eye on the smoke and the other on the road, but I came around another twisted bend and lost the smoke. Parking the Hummer under a nearby thicket off the road, I locked up and took off on foot once I strapped on my ankle pocket and secured my .25 caliber pistol. I worked my arm into my shoulder holster, loaded the Ruger, and secured it before taking a deep breath.

I crawled over several tip-ups, probably left by Hurricane Ivan when it ravaged Appalachia with floodwaters. I was amazed at the enormous root systems some of them had right on the side of a mountain. I climbed, pulling up on protruding rocks as I made my way. Hoisting myself up boulders created a hot mist all over my body, then the mountain gusts quickly chilled me.

I stood on the pinnacle of a mountain with nowhere to go but down. I tottered for a second before squatting and grabbing onto what few weeds I could grasp in my fingers. I sat down and eased my binoculars around enough to sight the smoke again. It appeared to be on the next mountain, which meant I'd have to go down in the valley and back up the other side.

Thirsty, I suddenly remembered the coffee I'd brought along, cold now, and back in the Hummer. I couldn't concern myself with that. I was too close to discovering an illegal still. I had to be alert for bootleggers who probably had a spotter, more than likely a kid who should be in school somewhere.

I moved my body over a few feet with my hands and found a tiny path through the thick brush. Slipping off my perch, I tried to inch down the mountain a little at a time, my toes curling into tight springs inside my boots, but kudzu snagged me, suspending me in air. I began to writhe and twist, my long stretched-out body getting more entwined with every move until I managed to topple out under it, only to pick up too much speed once my legs touched ground.

Now off-balance, I catapulted down the mountain, bracing for a nasty fall, but the fall never came. Once again kudzu clutched me and flung me into a green springy hammock of vines before dumping me out on the valley floor some yards below. I lay still a few seconds and made certain I had my guns and equipment. I checked for injuries. Fortunately I hadn't been thrown onto boulders.

Clouds gathered over the mountains in the distance. The binoculars weren't picking up any smoke at all. I had no idea which way to go.

I pulled out my radio and called for any agents who might be in the area. I got no local agent response. I knew better than to call the SRT; I'd never live it down.

Is this part of my initiation too?

I slapped my hand on the ground.

Who gives a shit about moonshine? In fact, if I had some, I'd have a swig right now.

A chill hit my skin and skittered away as I watched the rain coming. Sprinkles became drops and drops became plops. Plops became a curtain of heavy rain. I darted under a bulky kudzu canopy, the only shelter I had.

Even though the day was young, dark came with the storm. I had no recourse but to stay put until the rain and wind subsided, my bagel long gone and my lips parched. The rain came down relentlessly and settled in, no end in sight. I made myself a makeshift kudzu bed, wondering if I'd be strangled if I fell asleep.

~~~~~

Morning brought fog, and I awoke, damp and shivering. I checked my pockets for weapons and other gear I'd brought along on this poor excuse for an assignment.

What idiot came up with the idea of sending a new agent out alone in this terrain anyway?

I still wondered if this was an unofficial SBI initiation and if so, I was ready to laugh with them and get home to warmth and hot food. Then I realized my glasses only contained one lens.

The radio: a worthless piece of crap. And my cell phone? No good because no cellular tower existed anywhere I'd been in the last fifteen hours. I sighed. I crawled out from under the kudzu and looked around. It would be dangerous to go far in the dense fog. I'd have to literally feel my way along. But which way? I was totally disoriented.

I pulled myself by substantial branches and slogged along at turtle pace, having no idea where I was going. It was hopeless. I found a rock and sat, hugging myself to ward off any more chill. I snoozed until the cold mist made me shiver. I could see the sun through many layers of fog, trying its best to burn through.

"Come on, Big Guy, bring it on down."

Slowly the fog dissipated and I had more visibility even though everything around me was wet. I yanked my binoculars around and made a decision about which direction to take. My stomach gnawed. I tried to ignore it as I pushed on, over cliffs and down gulleys, hoping I wasn't getting deeper into trouble. If I could get to the highway, surely someone would come by who could take me to my Hummer. If. I didn't see any sign of a road anywhere, only boulders, trees, and caverns.

I continued on my slow trek until the sun shone straight over my head. Midday. I'd been out here for more than a day. And I had no idea if I was going toward the highway or farther away from it. I grabbed a bush to pull myself up on a rock, noticing long, hard thorns too late. I pulled back bloody fingers, extracted a few thorns, and wiped blood on my wet clothes. I was tired and careless. I moved around the rock and in another direction, wanting to find a high enough perch to see a road. Visibility should be great if I were high enough.

I saw a peak some distance away and worked my way through the mountain obstacle course to it. I pulled myself up on the boulder and looked around. With my Bushnells I found a road, back the way I'd just come. Disheartened, I climbed down and headed back, trying to keep my bearings and focus. The day faded away with astonishing swiftness as I realized I wasn't going to get out before dark.

~~~~~

A chipmunk scared me as badly as I scared it in the next dawn's light. I wanted shelter, dry clothes, and a hot meal. I followed the creature in what I hoped was the direction of my ride. I spotted a huge kudzu leaf full of water and drank it before moving toward the peak I hoped I'd scooted down the day before.

My tummy howled as I grabbed rocks and roots and worked my way to the top. I pulled out the binoculars and crouched to peer under brush and trees, finally spotting the copper Hummer a little farther away than I'd anticipated, but at least I could see it. Finally. I eased myself down, working out a plan a few degrees at a time. Near a small patch of flat ground I spotted it again and ran, tripping a few yards away—right into the anal glands of a skunk.

The damned striped fur bag threw its tail in reverse and soaked me with a pungent discharge. My eyes stung and my nostrils caved in while my mouth twisted and contorted, followed by the rest of my body.

I pulled my Ruger to shoot the little shit but couldn't see well enough to take aim. I couldn't wipe off since my clothes were saturated with revolting spew. Fumbling for keys, I unlocked the Hummer and grabbed the emergency blanket, wiping my eyes and face first. Stink dripped from my hair. I mopped. I peeled off all my clothes and wrapped nakedness in the blanket, careful to toss my guns and gear in the back as far from me as possible. I left the sturdy camo clothing and blue lace undies beside the road.

~~~~~

I blew the horn when I parked behind the Pathfinder. Taryn came to the door. I rolled down the window, and she waved and walked towards me.

"Taryn, stop!"

"What the hell? Oh, my God! You've been skunked!"

I nodded.

"Go around to the back porch, Logan. I'll fetch the hose-pipe." I left the Hummer doors opened to air out and tramped around to the back, dragging the blanket with me.

Taryn pulled the hose over near me. Before turning it on, she picked up a gallon jug and came at me with it. I pulled back.

"Tomato juice. I've got to do it, Logan. It's the only thing'll get the skunk off."

I stood still and held my breath as she poured the entire gallon of tomato juice over my head and down my long naked body.

"Open your eyes and take this brush to scrub with."

I obeyed. She snatched up the blanket, wadded it into a ball, and set it on fire.

"I have another one you can use," she assured me. "By the way, the hose water's cold." These words came at the same time the water, a few degrees shy of freezing, hit me.

"Th..th..thanks."

1

Becky Paul opened the music room early and walked in with her thermos of strong black coffee. She put her purse away, but he flipped on the lights and startled her. He felt a huge smile smear across his face. He'd been waiting for her.

"What on earth are you doing in here?" He noticed she didn't reciprocate his smile. They'd been divorced for years but he still appeared occasionally where she shopped, or one day at a pool where she'd taken her two daughters, Bea and Ally. He still loved her and enjoyed being near her, even if she was married to Steve Paul now. He didn't care much for Steve or the girls either.

"I was on my way by and just thought I'd pop in before your first class. How are you?" he grinned, walking closer. He knew better than to rush her or to touch her.

"Why're you here? Really? I have a private piano lesson before the bell rings. My student'll be here any second. You shouldn't be here. And I don't want you using your master key to come in here whenever you want to."

"I need to talk to you about something important, something that could affect the rest of your life," he announced. "I can come back later." He turned toward the door.

Becky said, "No. Don't come here anymore. You're supposed to check in at the office. I know you want to talk about getting back together. How many times have we had this conversation? It's over! I'm married, for Heaven's Sake! I have been for a long time. You know Steve and you've seen the girls. Let it go. Just get over it." Both of her hands were braced against the edge of the desk as if deliberately keeping it between them.

He shook his head, finally noticing a little girl standing in the door with a music book.

"Come in, Carrie," Becky said, motioning the child in.

He walked to the door and turned around. "They can't call the law on me, Becky. I work here. I have keys to every school in this county." He didn't tell her he'd been quietly fired from the school system, but had extra keys he didn't turn in. He pointed his index finger at his ex-wife. "We'll talk again, I promise you."

He stayed calm and in control, but noticed Becky shook by the time he moved beyond the doorway. He couldn't blame her, but it had been a lot of years since he'd walloped her. At least he wasn't yelling and being abusive now, the reason she left in the first place. He'd maintained his composure to show her he could stay in control. He'd changed. He had to find a way to convince her he could restrain himself and she'd be safe with him again.

•

Quit tryin' to protect your ma. Your such a piss ant. Your good for nothin'. See what you bore me, you whore? A worthless piece of shit!

8

Twenty-seven days later

He checked his watch. Becky was running late. She'd been detained in her school's music room by some asshole parent, and she'd have to walk into her master's course at Mars Hill College after her professor started the lecture. He knew Becky despised being late for anything. The drive from Trust to Mars Hill College—thirty-five miles through the mountain—and it took over an hour even on a clear night.

He knew she looked forward to the day she could leave Grange Elementary School behind and work with college students who loved the art and were as passionate about it as she was; she only had three more classes to complete.

It rained just enough that afternoon to make the mountain road treacherous, and he knew she'd have to deal with the fog when she started back home in the dark.

He'd called her after school, wanting to meet her somewhere, but she was already late and told him she didn't have time, so he hung up on her. Sometimes she really pissed him off. She had time for everybody but him. Nevertheless, he'd felt blessed to have met her years ago at the church where she played the organ. He'd joined the choir to spend more time with her even though he couldn't carry a tune in a long-bed truck. She'd changed his life. He was a better man around her. She had been a good influence.

A deer ran across the road in front of Becky, causing her to slam on the brakes. He figured if it had been dark, she would've hit it. He knew she was well aware most of this road had no guardrail and if she left the road, she'd be over the mountain's edge. But she seemed unaware he followed just far enough behind to keep her in sight.

Once class ended at nine, Becky stopped at a Quik Mart and got a Mountain Dew and a hotdog. She bought some gas and drove into the fog on the mountain he knew would make her tense.

Becky planned to get braces on her teeth the next day. She'd needed them since she was a little girl. Her front teeth protruded enough that she was called "Bugs" during her school years. Her family couldn't afford braces so she'd promised herself someday she'd have her teeth fixed. And he thought she contemplated a nose job if she could afford it. Her nose and teeth had never bothered him, but she was self-conscious. She'd set aside money for the master's degree, and the orthodontist, and finally, she'd set a goal for the nose. That was Becky. Goal-oriented. Focused.

Her Honda Accord sputtered and began to slow down just as she crossed Banjo Branch, a remote spot on Highway 213. It slowed to a crawl and stopped in the middle of the road. She'd try to crank it, of course, but it wouldn't even purr. He was certain of that. Too foggy to see a little shoulder on the road and she couldn't reach it any way.

His headlights were behind her. She switched on the hazard lights to signal distress. His truck came to a stop behind her. He got out and snatched her door open.

"My God, what are you doing here?" She looked up at him in shock.

He replied she was lucky he followed her.

"Why are you out here anyway? Did you have to go to Mars Hill for something?"

"Yeah."

"I guess that's just luck, huh?" He nodded. "I don't know what's happened to the car. Can you look? Someone will hit me if I stay in this road."

"Not too many folks out on a night like this. Just us fools." He lifted the hood with his thickly gloved hands and reattached the hoses he'd tampered with while she attended class. He made sure everything was back in place and turned to her as she sat in the driver's seat.

"Is it fixed?"

"I want to talk to you," he said, stepping to her opened door. "Becky, I love you. I've always loved you. You know that." His tone became a growl. "But don't you ever fuck with me!"

"What are you talking about? What do you mean?" A look of alarm spread over her face. "Wait a minute. Did you do something to my car?" He was silent.

"I'm talking to you! What's wrong?" she yelled at him, throwing a pitiful punch at his shoulder.

He grabbed her by her gold sweater and jerked her out of the car before she could reach for her cell phone. His face was inches from her nose and she trembled.

She shut her eyes, probably praying he'd drop her and leave. Instead he clenched his fist, and while holding her tiny body in his angry grasp, he felt his other gloved fist beat her in the face. The fist hit her and hit her until she stopped screaming and went limp in his arms. He saw the fists beat her, watched the whole thing, powerless to stop the assault on the woman he loved.

When the fists dropped her back into the seat, he realized she was so badly beaten most of her teeth were knocked out and others were pushed way past the gum line. He checked her pulse. None, not even a faint beat. He looked down. Blood was everywhere, all over the ground, spattered on the car, and soaked into the front seat.

He straightened Becky up in the seat and looked both ways to make certain no one drove up on them. He realized he'd made bloody shoe prints so he twisted his shoes several times in each one to make them impossible to identify.

When he felt he'd covered his tracks, he got into his truck and drove to an overlook miles away before stripping off all the blood-spattered clothes and pouring gasoline from the bed of the truck on them, including the old shoes and gloves. He threw the ashes and remnants of the soles over the rail into impenetrable kudzu.

Why had she made him do it? It was all her fault. How could he have hurt the woman he loved? She wasn't a beauty, but inside, no finer woman existed than Becky. He wept.

•

You're a wuss! Rubbish from the git go. You'll never amount to a pile of horseshit! Quit tryin' to squirm away. I ain't turnin' you loose 'til I'm done with ya.

9

Haze DeBrew was almost finished with the built-in four-poster bed he built for Mrs. Rasmussen. He prided himself in doing quality work. That's how he'd kept his reputation in the western part of the state as one of the best woodworkers anywhere. He put the finishing touches on the beveled posts with his spoke shave before tucking it back into his toolbox. He decided to do some extra wiring she wanted done so he wouldn't have to make another trip to Tennessee. He tried to stay within a fifty-mile radius of his house but this project was lucrative enough to pull him a little farther out. Mrs. Rasmussen said money would be no object and that she wanted the best it could buy.

Tired after hours of tedious handwork, he hurriedly picked up the claw hammer he'd used to put the bed together and prepared to hit one last nail that didn't suit him. Haze was on the downswing when a log truck went by and backfired, distracting him long enough to hit himself in the knuckles. Blood spattered. Pain followed. He'd need stitches.

Mrs. Rasmussen rushed to him with her first-aid kit and applied peroxide and iodine, followed by a bandage covered with yards of gauze and tape. He thanked her, picked up his sizable check, closed up the toolbox, and crawled into the truck. He drove into Newport and found Medic-Quik.

Stitched and bandaged correctly, he drove to a liquor store and bought a half-gallon of Wild Turkey before beginning his rainy trek back through the mountains to grog out on pain medicine and booze.

He needed to drink away the memories and hurt anyway. Becky. His Becky. Dead. How could it have happened? Dead. He couldn't accept it. It had to be a nightmare. He slammed his hurt hand on the steering wheel.

Eeyow!

No, he was awake and Becky was dead. He loved her so much. Why would anyone want to hurt her? She was as gentle as any human he'd ever met. Far more gentle than anyone around him growing up. Becky. The life beaten out of her. Gone. Forever. Tears poured down his face as he drove on, promising to drink himself into unconsciousness.

~~~~~

He pulled himself up from the sofa he'd spent the night on and staggered to the kitchen. His hand throbbed; his heart was coming through the palm of his hand. He looked intently into it, half way expecting it to rupture any second.

He didn't even remember driving home. It was a miracle he'd made it on those narrow winding roads by the giant Busch plant and through Pisgah National Forest in the fog. He stopped in front of the refrigerator and glanced at his reflection in its stainless steel door. What the...? He was covered with red clay. He looked down at his arms, his jeans, back at his face. What the hell had he done while he was stoned?

He stared at his arms and tried to remember, running his hands through his butch hair. Some girl walking up the frigging mountain road about to get run over. Hadn't he stopped and let her climb in? She kept telling him she'd just been hired by some school system to troubleshoot computers. She was lost, apparently didn't have a car. Or somebody'd left her motor-mouth ass out there alone.

He'd had no idea why she was walking and where she was going. He couldn't remember. She was pretty wasted too, the best he could remember. And she had diarrhea of the mouth. He remembered wanting her to shut up. He held his throbbing head in his good hand a few seconds before walking back to the sofa and collapsing into a gluey state.

When he came to, he eased around the house, hoping to stop the throbbing hand and head. It didn't work. He walked out the back door and down to the waterfall a mile and one-fourth away in the Pisgah Forest. The mist always refreshed him. This time would be no different. He lay back and let the dampness cover his face and sober the rest of his body.

Once his head eased off, he hiked back to the house, stopping at his truck bed. He noticed his shovel, covered with clay. He froze. He had to remember. Where had the clay come from? Had he done something to the girl? His eyes bulged.

Wait a minute. Think! Think!

No, that couldn't be right. He knew he didn't. He couldn't have done that. He knew sometimes he couldn't remember things after a drunk, but he'd remember something like that, wouldn't he? The realization of what he'd done hit and he threw his hand over his mouth, but not fast enough to stop the erupting vomit.

•

I tol you you cain't handle it. You're a coward. Your cryin' makes me puke. You cain't do nothin' right!

10

Chase Railey walked into the Trust General Store and Grill and headed straight for me, alone, reading a map in a corner.

"Agent Hunter! May I join you?" Chase asked, already sliding into the opposite side of the booth. I knew why he was here.

"How are you?" I sipped my coffee. Chase motioned for the waitress, who seemed especially interested in serving him. She hurried over, eyelashes fluttering over her citron eyes, to pour him a cup and refill mine.

"Good morning, Chase," said the waitress who was, without a doubt, Cherokee. Her messy raven hair fell down to her shoulder blades, the kind of messy that looks sexy. Her eyes drank in Chase with a thirst I couldn't ignore. Her skin was gorgeous and her lips were pouty. She exuded sex.

"Hi ya, Raina." He winked. She blushed.

He ordered two sunny-side-up eggs, country ham, fried green tomatoes, grits, and biscuits with sawmill gravy. My scrambled eggs, bacon, and grits arrived about the same time his buffet did. Raina hovered over Chase a few seconds longer than I thought necessary.

"How've you been? How's the cabin? You still live alone?"

Chase looked somewhat embarrassed. "Uh, good, Raina. The cabin's good, and yes, I still live in it."

She touched his hand lightly with her fingertips. "I'd love to see it again. When are you gonna call me?" She whispered something close to his ear.

Chase cleared his throat in obvious discomfort. "Please excuse us, Raina. This is business."

She gave me a wicked look and headed for the kitchen. "Sure."

"How's the moonshine search going?" Chase asked with a nervous grin. He cut a small piece of fried tomato and put it on my plate. "Gotta try these. You easterners don't know what's good for breakfast." He winked, not mentioning the scene with Raina. They obviously had a past.

"Thanks. I'm getting nowhere fast," I responded, adjusting my glasses so I could see him even better. "Thick and difficult terrain. I haven't even gotten warm, but I've seen a lot of mountains and kudzu. I'm pretty frustrated with this assignment." I didn't mention the skunk as I tried the fried tomato.

"*You're* frustrated?" His tone of voice changed. "Logan, may I call you Logan?" I nodded. "I need your help," he leaned forward and whispered. "I'm sure you've heard about the other murder. I still haven't made any headway with John Roman's investigation, and now Becky Paul is dead. I'd just sat down to eat a late supper when the sheriff called and said Becky'd had a wreck up near Banjo Branch. A hysterical motorist called it in. I went to the scene and, believe me, it was no accident, the worst beating I've ever seen. She was so tiny; she didn't stand a damned chance.

"I can't figure out why she stopped in the middle of that dark foggy road and got out. She'd know how dangerous that was. I've known Steve and Becky for years, even before they were married," Chase continued. I remained attentive. He wore a crisp light-blue dress shirt and a navy tie filled with swirls of color. My gaze moved to his blond wavy hair and the mesmerizing but upset tanzanite eyes.

"I talked with the two troopers and we checked everything we could in the dark and fog. The car had plenty of gas. Nothing seemed wrong under the hood either. I checked the belts and oil. Blood was everywhere. She must've been attacked when she got out of the car. I searched for tracks with my spotlight but they were all smeared intentionally."

"Was she on the road?"

"No, she was beaten outside the car and set back in her seat. Her teeth were all out except for the ones embedded in her gums. Dead when I got there. The lab guy found fibers in her mouth. He's analyzing them. Probably glove fibers.

"There's little traffic when it's foggy and few places to pull off the road. I can't imagine lying in wait for a car on that road late at night. It just doesn't make any sense."

"Maybe somebody followed her."

"Possibly. Look, as you're probably aware, our sheriff's department is small and inexperienced in murder. Sheriff Yandle told me last night he was going to call the SBI. I told him we already had an agent in the area and I'd try to find you. Logan, will you help us?"

My pulse raced because the gorgeous face across from me was irresistible and because I'd love to get involved in the murder investigation.

"I'll have to call Kent Poletti and see if he'll change my assignment. This *is* more urgent. I warn you, though, I've only investigated one murder case," I admitted.

"Did you get your man?" Chase questioned.

"Eventually," I answered without going into detail about my friend Pepper's millionaire lover, murdered at Genesis Beach. "I've just completed some criminalist training so I have more investigative knowledge than I did on that case."

"Criminalist, huh? I took a course too—really just an overview. I didn't realize you were one."

"I'm not. It's hard to explain. They seldom carry guns or make arrests, and they don't mess with dead bodies. They collect and analyze evidence in the lab. I want to be where the action is. Even though I'm not a criminalist, it helps to know how the process works. It makes my senses keener and makes me a better investigator, I think." He smiled at my obvious excitement about my job. "I want to know as much as possible and every case is different. I want to be valuable—no, indispensable," I emphasized.

"I'm sure you are," Chase whispered across the table. I shoveled in some eggs and watched Chase finish off his grits. He popped in the last bite of tomato and downed his last drop of coffee, waving Raina away with her offer of a refill.

"Chase, give me a call sometime, huh?"

"See you, Raina," he responded, leaving far more than an average tip.

Chewing on a toothpick, he leaned toward me. "I guess you're wondering how I can eat like a horse. I tend to eat when I'm stressed, and I never ate last night."

I understood. And he'd have plenty of opportunity to work off the calories before he got a chance to eat again.

I offered to follow him to the Sheriff's Department to see if we could piece together any details about the two cases.

"I was relieved somebody else told Steve about Becky. I went by later and sat with him a few minutes. He's totally torn up. One of the relatives swept the two girls away to Asheville until Steve can pull himself together. I talked him out of going to view the body. It won't be released for a while. We'll need to question Becky's professor and classmates, I guess, up at Mars Hill. They'd be the last to see her alive."

"Except for the killer," I added. "How old are the girls?"

"I think three and six."

We both shook our heads in dismay.

"I went by your place early this morning, or I should say Taryn's. Too upset to sleep. I hoped your light would be on. It wasn't, so I drove on to my cabin and stared at the woods until daybreak." Chase shuffled his feet. "We haven't solved Roman's murder. And now, another one, even more violent."

~~~~~

The smell of dirt curled through my nostrils as I rode past field after field of freshly plowed earth. Small farms all over Madison County had at least one cow and one outdated tractor. Some farmers still used the no till method of planting a new crop right over the old one. I wasn't sure why.

Clothes dried in the mountain breeze, flapping on the clotheslines attached from one pole to another across backyards. Most folks saw no need for a dryer, the mountain breeze worked just fine. In snow or ice, or on rainy days, they used drying racks made from wood they'd turned themselves. These people were self-sufficient. They had to be, and if the economy didn't stabilize soon, many more of us would have to learn to be self-sufficient.

I took the next switchback easier than Chase, who sped ahead of me. I slowed down to get a good look at a weathered barn—not the barn itself, but the quilt block in the middle of it where a loft door should be. Fascinated, I pulled over on the grass in front of it, absorbing the vibrant colors that more than likely told a story about this community and its people. I didn't know if folks other than Taryn continued to sew together cloth cut into specific designs, but these metal signs no doubt brought back a touch of Appalachian quilting history. As I drove on, I saw several more quilt blocks on barns and made a mental note to ask Taryn about them.

~~~~~

When we arrived at the Sheriff's department I noticed several rooms, the largest with desks backed up to each other, each with its own personal gooseneck lamp for long hours of tedious paperwork. I followed Chase past several deputies to a private office.

Sheriff Yandle stood.

"Agent Hunter, I've already called Kent Poletti and asked for your help. He'll be calling you," obese Sheriff Yandle said, stuffing the rest of a crème-filled doughnut in his mouth. He was almost as wide as he was tall, and something about his face reminded me of the Tasmanian devil.

"It's been twenty-eight days since the custodian died. We haven't found out a gall darn thing. Now we have a woman beaten to death. I don't know what's going on. The cases aren't alike in any way, so I guess it's just a coincidence."

"The cases are certainly different, sheriff. A man suffocated, what we call a soft kill. The woman beaten to death, lots of violence and blood, what we call a hard kill. It doesn't fit a serial profile. It's possible, I suppose, but not probable. Hopefully there won't be any more," I stated.

A deputy tossed Chase a package.

"Careful," another called out. "You'll break the contents." Chase opened the box, grinned, and pulled out four homemade chocolate macadamia cookies and set the box down for the others to devour. They were on them like hot butter on popcorn. I gave him a questioning look.

"My mom sends me a box of homemade goodies about once a month. I share."

I walked with him to his office, away from the main hub, where he obviously spent many hours: a sizable desk stacked with paper in every possible position, a small lamp, a couple of file cabinets that looked like discards, and little else.

A deputy appeared. Chase looked up at the grinning officer. "Logan, I promised to introduce you to this salivating deputy who's in love with your Hummer. Roy Nesbitt, Agent Logan Hunter."

He shook my hand vigorously. I told him he could look it over if he wanted to. I had the keys.

I bit into a cookie as my cell phone rang. Poletti was on the other end. "Hunter, since you're already in the mountains, and you've had some experience with murder, I'm transferring you from moonshine to murder. I'll assign another agent to moonshine. Let me know if you need more help. Keep me informed and be safe," and Poletti hung up.

I glanced at Chase, shoveling in the rest of the cookie. "I'm on the case."

Chase grinned, handing me another one, which I wrapped in a napkin and tucked into my pocket.

"Great! Let's start with Roman. I want you to see the pictures." He pushed the envelope across the desk.

I pulled the pictures out and adjusted my glasses so I could see through the one lens I had left. I looked at the picture of the trash bag with vapor on the inside from John Roman's last breaths of life. A zoom shot showed scratches on the inside of the bag we assumed were the custodian trying to claw his way out before he suffocated. Another showed his fingernails with tiny particles of plastic trash bag under them. I scanned others, mostly of John Roman's face with the life gone from it. The last shot showed the side of Roman's head, bearing a dark contusion, apparently from a blunt object.

"There's no doubt he was alive when he was put in the bag. He apparently spent his last few breaths trying to get out. What a horrible way to die," I said after close scrutiny.

"I'm interviewing some students at the school again. I'm not getting anywhere with it, though. It's like whoever did it is getting away free and clear. It gripes my ass." Chase stomped his foot and shook his wavy blonde hair.

I watched him closely as we walked out to the Hummer. He had the most kissable mouth I'd ever seen. Everything about this man interested me.

"Maybe the kids didn't do it, Chase. Hop in, and let's talk to these students together."

I didn't have to ask twice. Chase climbed in the passenger side and buckled up, grinning like a little schoolboy at Roy Nesbitt, who looked envious.

"I've never even sat in one of these. Now I get to ride," he said and we both laughed.

"Where'd you get it?"

"A friend gave it to me."

"Some friend."

Yes, Pepper Ellis was a dear and treasured friend. We'd been through so much together. I got the Hummer by default, really, and still felt uncomfortable with the idea. When Pepper's millionaire lover was murdered, she inherited everything: the furnished mansion at the beach, the yacht, too many vehicles to mention, and major stock in his million-dollar spa tub enterprise. She'd insisted on giving the Hummer to me as a gift when I lost my home and car in a hurricane while investigating his murder. She said it suited an SBI agent. I owed her an ovary.

On the way to Dulcimer High School, Chase filled me in on whom he'd questioned and how the investigation had stalled. If anyone knew anything, they weren't talking. He didn't like questioning teenagers because they tend to cover for their friends, or they're scared of retaliation. His phone rang.

"Hey, Mom. Yes, I got the cookies," he said, winking at me. "They're delicious. Supper? I doubt it. I'm working on two murder cases. Right now? I'm riding in a Hummer. Yeah, for real!" He laughed. "Catch you later. Love you too."

The fact he and his mother were close pleased me. I smiled through the windshield just as the school sign came into view: orange with black letters and the school's mascot, a long-legged moose wearing football cleats.

Students were changing classes. I parked near the end of the visitors' parking area to draw as little attention as possible. I needn't have bothered. Heads came around every corner and some male students walked out toward us, until, hearing the bell, they turned and ran, using a few choice profanities in the process.

"I guess I should've driven my old Jeep. You're creating a disturbance with this Hummer," Chase teased, leaning over and staring at me.

"What?"

"Are you aware that a lens is missing from your glasses?"

"Yes, and it's a long story."

11

Janah Zack stood in the front lobby where we entered.

"Dr. Zack, you've met Logan Hunter."

I stuck out my hand.

"It's good to see you again, Agent Hunter." She touched my sleeve. "Are you aware one of your lenses is missing?"

Chase tried to squelch a snicker.

"Oh, yes. I have to find time to get it replaced or get contacts."

"I love my contacts," she said, leading us back to her inner office. "Please come in. I'd like to talk with you both before any students do, if you don't mind," Janah said almost in a whisper.

She closed the door and offered us both the blue plaid loveseat in front of her desk. I hadn't noticed it on our previous visit. Chase watched for my reaction to having to sit snuggly beside him. We hadn't been so close before. It didn't bother me at all and I plopped down and pulled out my Palm Pilot. Chase pulled out his small notepad and a pencil.

"I appreciate your coming and we'll be cooperative. I have to admit, though, I'm upset that no progress has been made in John's death." Janah apparently believed in saying what she meant and meaning what she said.

"We are too, and that's why I'm glad to have Agent Hunter on the case with me now, Dr. Zack. I guess you've heard about the other murder, a music teacher at Grange Elementary."

"I did hear about it. I didn't know Mrs. Paul, but I heard she was a wonderful person. Do you think the same person—no, not a person—the same monster did both?" Janah asked, leaning over the desk.

"At this time we believe these are separate incidences, Dr. Zack. The similarity is they were both employed by the school system, but I suppose the school system is one of the largest employers in the county," I stated.

"The largest, I'd guess, since the textile mills closed."

"We'd like to go back over some questions you've already been asked, Dr. Zack," Chase added.

"I suppose so. But, I want this case solved fast, detectives. My entire school is stirred up, the teachers and the students. My maids. I can't get them to settle down. We're having more discipline problems than ever. It's just unsettling to all of us."

"We're doing the best we can with both murders, Dr. Zack," I said a little sternly. "An investigation of this type demands thoroughness. We can't rush and take the chance of being careless."

I asked her if she'd learned of any enemies John Roman had. She explained again about the teacher, Ella Goforth, who had seen some students giving Roman the finger at a ballgame and cursing him as they walked away. No one else reported any problems with John. We'd reviewed the school's surveillance tapes and Chase and I determined the headlights probably belonged to the murderer's full-sized truck. We shared what little information we could with Dr. Zack.

Chase and I spent several hours interviewing students about the ballgame and any other instances where students "dissed" Roman, as they called it. We learned several freshman couples had moved over to an unlit corner of the stadium to make out. They all said Mr. Roman came over and told them to go back to the bleachers in the lighted area.

Tait Glott admitted he shot Mr. Roman the bird as they walked off. "I made fun of him sometimes, but so did everybody else. He tried to do the principal's job and we didn't appreciate it. If Zack had a problem with us, why didn't she come over and run us off? It was none of JoJo's business."

"JoJo?"

"That's what the students called him. JoJo."

"Rather disrespectful, don't you think? So you resented him."

He shrugged. "Maybe. I don't know, detective. All's I know is I didn't kill him, and I don't know who did. We get blamed for everything around here. It ain't fair."

"We who?"

"Us, our crowd. We don't play football and the girls don't cheer. So we're not jocks. We don't make great grades so we're not geeks. We're in the middle, the forgotten. The easily blamed."

"Geez, that's the saddest story I've ever heard," Chase scowled, close to Tait's nose. "But, really, I need the names of everyone you hang with."

"Come on, man," whined Tait. "I ain't rattin' on nobody. Nobody done anything to that man. Anybody sayin' we did is a liar."

"I don't think you're telling us everything. That's obstruction of justice and I could arrest you."

"Arrest me? But I didn't do anything to that man! You'd have to arrest half the student body if you're charging me with disrespect."

I could understand why Chase hadn't made much progress. If the students knew more, they weren't saying. Tait, the obvious spokesman for the group, intimidated them. We decided to let the students go but promised to return. They were to get in touch with us if their memories improved.

We walked out to the area where John died and looked around again. I took a few digital pictures, but too much time and traffic had obliterated the crime scene, even though the yellow tape remained along with many rotten flower memorials. I asked about the trashcan and plastic the victim was in, and Chase said the killer left no fingerprints or blood to trace.

"There's no evidence of a struggle around the scene, so I assume Roman got caught off guard. Probably knocked out or dazed and wrapped in plastic. I rummaged through the Dumpster after the body left. The killer cleaned up well. No weapon found, although there was blunt-object trauma according to the coroner. Still, he said a blow to the head hadn't killed Roman. He'd suffocated in the plastic. The coroner ruled asphyxiation."

"I want to take a look at the collected evidence. Just in case something was overlooked." Chase glanced at me. "No offense."

Chase made a note. "None taken."

We walked toward the Hummer while two girls approached us.

"Can we help you?"

"I guess so," one responded, looking nervous and anxious. The other girl nudged her to talk. "Are you a real SBI agent?"

"Yes." I flashed my badge.

"Cool!"

I smiled. "Was there something else?"

"Meg and me were in the locker room one morning when a man got caught for peeking at us from the janitor's closet."

"Mr. Roman?" I asked.

"No ma'am. See, Meg, I told you this didn't have nothing to do with Mr. Roman at all."

Meg reddened.

I coaxed the talker. "Look...ah, what's your name?"

"Sorry. Ashland. Ashland Lawrence. Anyways we were changing in the locker room when we all heard a loud noise from the closet. Sara Jane and Ruthie opened the door and one of the maintenance men glared at us. The school deputy dragged him to the office and we heard he got fired. It wasn't Mr. Roman. He wouldn't do nothing like that. Some of us were talking and thought you might need to know since Mr. Roman had to do everything by himself after that other man got fired."

"How long between the time this man got caught and Mr. Roman's death?"

The girls put their heads together and figured about a month. I made a note.

"We had planned to talk with you girls anyway. About the home baseball game."

"Yeah, Tait said you were questioning him about it," Ashland said.

"Tell us what happened at the game," Chase coaxed.

"Meg, you tell them."

"Me? Why me? You were out there, too!" The girls scowled at each other.

"Look," I said touching her on the shoulder, "I don't know what's going on, but we want some answers. If you don't want to talk with us, we'll call your parents and get them to join us, but we will get the information one way or another."

"No!" yelled Ashland. "Please don't do that. I mean..."

"What exactly do you mean, Ashland?" The girls glanced at each other.

"My mother told me not to get off the bleachers. I wasn't supposed to be walking around with Tait."

"Me either," added Meg.

"Ladies, I'm tired of this!" Chase stomped the ground, having lost all patience. "Spill you guts and do it now!"

"Okay, sir. We, Ashland and I, walked around at the game with Tait and Scott. They're not our boyfriends, just somebody to walk around with, you know."

"Get to the part about Mr. Roman."

"We went around the track and over to the trash dump to throw away our chili cheese trays and drink cups. Mr. Roman came barreling over to fuss at us. He said we had no business over there, and to get back over to the bleachers."

"Why would he fuss at you for throwing trash away?"

"Because that's off limits for students. Some have been caught making out behind the Dumpster."

"And you weren't making out with the boys?"

Ashland and Meg stared holes through the ground. I decided to answer the question myself. "So, Mr. Roman ran you off for making out with Tait and Scott. Then what?" The girls both blushed but kept quiet. I eased closer. "Spit it out."

"Okay! We were, but please don't tell our parents."

"I want to know what happened next."

"We started back toward the bleachers, but Tait wouldn't shut up. He called Mr. Roman some ugly names and shot him the bird." *Freaking finally!*

"That wasn't so hard, was it?" My sarcasm carried a nasty tone. "What did Mr. Roman do then?"

"He didn't do nothing. He never said a word to Tait. He just watched us go and headed off in another direction."

"Did you dislike Mr. Roman?"

"No," the girls said in unison. Then Meg added, "He just tried to act like the principal. He did more than he's supposed to do for a janitor."

"Ever stop to think he might be trying to help the principal? Like another set of eyes and ears?" They stared without speaking.

We thanked them and decided to go back by Dr. Zack's office. I didn't know about Chase, but that exchange made me feel frazzled. I felt like I'd just wrestled a bobcat.

We found the principal in the cafeteria supervising lunch lines, so we decided to eat a school lunch and wait for her. The options: chicken nuggets or pizza that looked like road kill. We chose the nuggets and fries along with a small side salad. I still wasn't sure the nuggets contained chicken, but the food stopped the hunger.

Dr. Zack joined us at a table near the end of dinner period. "How was it?"

"Surprisingly good," I remarked. "I never cared much for school food but this is satisfactory."

"It used to taste better, but in order to provide healthier food, all the lard and good stuff I grew up on have been cut out. The flavor's gone, but it's supposed to be more nutritious," she explained. "Let's go back to my office."

We walked beside her through the blue English hall and red science hall and approached the corner at her office door. I backed up around the science hall to catch another glimpse of the bulletin board I'd noticed. I took off my glasses long enough to see it clearly. Across the top of it: HOW I GOT LAID. That certainly got my attention. I read beneath this sign the story of how an egg is formed and hatched by a bird, signed by Hen Egg. Somewhat relieved, I caught up with the others.

"Dr. Zack," Chase began, "we have more questions. As you know, we've talked to students. We understand a maintenance man was fired shortly before John Roman died."

Janah Zack straightened up in her chair. "Why, yes, but what's that got to do with John's murder?"

"We're not sure of any connection, but we need the details. We need to know every possible incident, whether you think it relates or not," I said.

"I'm sorry. I didn't mean to withhold information. We're a small school so our custodial staff is limited. We rely on the county to send someone to help with repairs and regular maintenance John didn't have time to do or didn't know how to do.

"We had a wonderful worker who could do just about anything. Talented. He'd even paint some halls on the weekends so they'd be dry by Monday morning."

"How did this man get along with Roman?"

"I never heard any complaints. When I saw them together, they were fine and usually ate dinner together. Sometimes they'd even share a laugh. I really don't think he'd have any reason to hurt John."

"Why did you fire him?"

She twisted her shoulders in discomfort. "Technically the school system fired him, but I initiated the process after we caught him peeping at some girls in the locker room. He'd drilled little holes in the door. It seemed obvious he'd

drilled them since his drill was in his truck. He denied it
though. He said the holes were already there and he just
took advantage of them."

"Did he give you any trouble when you fired him?"

"No, he really didn't. I had a deputy beside me and, of
course, Scott Klixx was involved, but no, he went right to
his truck. I sent John to get his keys."

"So the man didn't leave with any keys that could give
him access to this school later?"

"No, he handed the whole ring of keys to John and we
checked to make certain we had them all. A few keys that
didn't belong to our particular school were sent back to
central maintenance. I reported the incident to the
superintendent, who immediately terminated him from the
school system."

"What was this man's name?" I prepared to write it in
my PDA.

"Haze DeBrew."

"Do you know if he found another job?"

"I really don't have any idea, Agent Hunter. You might
check with our central office to see if anyone has requested
information on him. The word doesn't always get around. I
understand he has a lucrative business on the side anyway.
You know, carpentry, electrical, and even plumbing, I think.
Again, I'm sorry I didn't tell you this in the beginning. It's
so hard to remember everything."

12

Chase and I headed for Steve Paul's house to find out all we could about the night Becky died. The standard white pedestal of flowers stood on the front porch to signify a death. Chase walked me up to a tall, sandy-haired man with a beleaguered face being consoled by some ladies with arms full of casseroles. They walked on into the house and Chase hugged the distraught man.

"Steve, this is a friend of mine, Logan Hunter. Do you feel up to talking to us a minute in private?"

Steve Paul walked by us to a nearby clearing, just gazing at the field beyond as he trembled. Chase told him I worked for the SBI.

"SBI? We need the SBI?"

"Steve, you have to remember we have another murder that hasn't been solved, and we're not experienced like Agent Hunter."

Steve reached for my hand and held it, aiming his bloodshot eyes at mine. His grief made him appear much older than his thirty-five years.

"Agent Hunter, find him. Find the bastard who did this to my Becky," Steve pleaded. He turned to Chase. "I...I don't know what to tell the girls. How am I supposed to raise two little girls alone? We were so happy. Becky looked forward to finishing her master's degree. She only had a few more classes. She was good to everybody. It just doesn't make any sense."

"Mr. Paul, did your wife ever mention having trouble with anybody? Could she have an enemy you weren't aware of? Maybe someone at her school or in a graduate class with her?" I asked.

"You didn't know my Becky, but I can assure you she didn't have enemies. Of course, I don't know the people in her graduate class, but I think she'd have told me if she felt uncomfortable with any of them."

"Do you know Haze DeBrew, Mr. Paul?" His face reddened.

Chase grabbed my arm. "Not now, Logan." I pulled away.

"Mr. Paul?" I looked straight at him to avoid Chase's glare.

"Yeah. Yes, Agent Hunter, of course. He's Becky's ex. Why? Do you think he had something to do with this?"

"I'm just asking, Mr. Paul. How did they get along?"

"Too well to suit me."

"What does that mean?" Chase asked.

"Becky still saw him occasionally. She didn't hate him. I think she felt sorry for him."

He walked back toward the house, stopped, and sobbed as though he'd never be able to stop. "They won't release her body."

"These things take time, Steve," Chase said. We gave him space and stayed quiet. He eventually went into the house and got his wife's address and phone book and brought it out to me. He said all her contacts were in it. We thanked him and left as cars and trucks filled the yard and roadside.

Night approached by the time I dropped Chase off to get his Jeep. He asked if Taryn would let him in if he came over later to go through the book with me. I told him I'd asked her not to shoot him.

Taryn was glad to see me when I got home. She'd made some chicken salad and cut up some apples to go with it. I asked if she minded Chase coming over.

"Lord, no, child, that fine-looking hunk is welcome in my house any time!" she exclaimed and we both laughed, Taryn's laugh, loud and contagious.

"We'll be quiet. We need to go through Becky Paul's address book and contact people tomorrow morning."

We ate in silence, both of us thinking about the two murders. I liked Taryn. She wasn't after me to tell her about my work; she said she wasn't going to interfere and so far she'd kept her word.

"By the way, the bureau transferred me to the murders, in case you were wondering how I got involved." I felt I owed her an explanation.

"I'm so glad, Logan. Everybody around here is upset. The worst thing I can remember? A suicide some years ago, and tragic enough," Taryn said as she rose from the table, shaking her platinum head. She offered me an apple and I took it for later. Her reading glasses fogged over and she snatched them off her face.

"Don't worry, Logan, I don't intend to run naked in the yard while Chase is here," she said, raising an eyebrow at me. "You rest and I'll clean this up. I'm fixing to go to my bedroom to finish reading a raunchy new book I've got," she stated, laughing at my reaction.

"Raunchy?"

"Yeah, I may even have to take two cold showers." I giggled. "The house is yours. If you go out early in the morning, just leave me a note so I won't fix breakfast. I have an early meeting before school myself. Oh, and my friend Ceil and I are going out to supper I reckon. We do that at least once a month. You'll meet her. Her son is a deputy but I seldom see him. He's not a detective like Chase."

I've met him, haven't I?

I decided to take a short walk, going out the porch door into the misty evening as it dampened the field of wildflowers and posh foliage. I didn't recognize all of them but I noticed the yellow buttercups and crabapple blossoms that signaled spring. I touched the bright yellow witch hazel blooms and moved on to the lush green Bear Brush, white Milk Maids, and powder blue Hound's Tongue.

I'm not sure how far I ventured before I sensed him and froze—and he froze. Through the mist I saw him perk up his thick ears. His eyes were two slits, keenly taking in my presence. His mouth curved into what seemed a grin. A wolf. A sizeable wolf. A predatory wolf. My heart propelled fear through my ear canals and past the eardrums, muffling all sounds other than its *kthunk-kthunk*. He stood statuesque and proud in the field of wildflowers. Our gazes stayed fixed on each other until a gossamer fog settled over us. Even as I kept both eyes on him, he disappeared.

The encounter unsettled my nerves. I eased my way back to Taryn's porch, sensing him still nearby. Waiting perhaps. Waiting for me to make a mistake. I eased back to the screened door and moved inside, deciding to shower the ominous feeling off before Chase came.

~~~~~

When I heard the heavy brass doorknocker, I went to greet him in jeans and tee shirt with bare feet.

"Where are your glasses?"

"I just showered. But I can see without them. I wear them more for weak eye muscles than for vision." He nodded at my explanation. "But, I'm really tired of them. I need to get contacts when I have time." I sauntered past him.

"I haven't touched the book. I waited to go through it with you. I don't know any of them but you might." I took him to the porch and offered him the leather chair while I flopped into the overstuffed one.

"I talked to the SBI lab and they're doing a mitochondria DNA of Becky's hair and bones, but it'll take thirty to sixty days to find out if the guy left traces. They did say the fibers were cotton work gloves. And they're commonly sold at hardware stores across America. Probably every man in North Carolina has at least one pair."

I put the address book on the weathered table between us. Chase picked it up, opened it to the first entries, and thumbed through the family, friends, and associates listed. "Aunt Mavis, Uncle Norman, Janet Langley, Barbara Hall, Margaret Tucker, Marie Downey." The ones he recognized as family he passed over for the moment. He let his finger move through the list of friends, most of whom he didn't know. Among them, though, was a name he did recognize, Haze DeBrew, her ex-husband.

"This is interesting," Chase pointed out. "She's listed her ex, Haze DeBrew, as a friend, not family. I guess that's normal, huh?"

"Well, he wouldn't be family. Steve said she felt sorry for him. At least he's listed as a friend and not an enemy."

"Dr. Zack fired him, but she didn't indicate any problem between him and John Roman. He's a master carpenter, electrician, and handy man. He does all kinds of odd jobs for people. He's good. Probably the best within seventy-miles," Chase announced.

"Taryn mentioned him. I think he did some carpentry work to this house. We may want to talk with him to see just what kind of relationship he had with his ex-wife and John Roman. I'm putting him in my PDA as a possible suspect, although we don't really have anything we can pen on him," I said. "Has he married again?"

"I don't know."

"We'll find out. And Becky Paul's husband will become a suspect simply because spouses go on the list anyway. Did he stand to gain a large sum of money? Were they bickering?"

I glanced at Chase whose face contorted.

"People aren't always what they seem. Maybe you didn't know Becky or Steve as well as you thought you did. We have to ask the tough questions." I tried to take the edge off his barbed expression. "I don't know these folks, but you do. It's going to be tougher for you to interrogate them. I'll be glad to do it."

Chase glowered at me.

"I mean, you said you were friends with Becky and Steve Paul. But how well do you really know them? Could they have had marital problems? Could she have been cheating on Steve with her ex?"

"Geez! Where is this coming from, Logan?" Chase hopped up and walked to the porch door. "My God, how can you make such statements?"

"Do I detect battery acid in your voice?"

He whirled around. "What?"

"Chase, I'm not the bad guy. And I have to ask the hard questions. If you know some of these people, maybe the sheriff needs to assign—"

"Don't even go there!" His red face was inches from my nose. I decided to keep my trap shut in case he thought of biting my nose off.

He backed away, a strange look inching over his face. He combed his blond wavy hair with his fingers, and turned away from me.

"I know you're not the bad guy. I understand what you're saying, but Becky didn't seem the type to cheat. She and Steve adored each other as far as I know. But, then again, I'm not really that close to them anymore." He pointed a finger at me. "You're right. I guess I don't know them that well. And this is my case—well, yours and mine now. So, what's the plan?" I gathered quick thoughts and stayed calm. I didn't want a repeat performance of temper, or tension, or whatever the hell that was.

"We need to talk to teachers at her school, her professor, the people in this book, and we have to ask DeBrew if he has an alibi for that night. We'll talk to Steve again in a few days." Chase agreed.

We decided to get some rest before we started out early in the morning. I walked him to his Jeep and watched him leave. The mountain fog set in and left an ominous feeling that Trust was full of tension and danger.

I'd heard the wolf and couldn't sleep. I eased out to the screened porch and wrapped up in an afghan in the chair, and stared into the fog. My imagination played tricks on me.

Is he there? Why is he hanging around?

I decided I wasn't afraid of him, but I had a healthy respect for the creature. He was beautiful. I wanted to see him again, to get a better look at him, but preferably in daylight.

Thoughts raced through my head about the murders, about what made the killer tick, about Chase Railey. I sat still, half-conscious, until around three in the morning when a soft rain stirred me and I dragged myself back to bed.

13

I headed to Mars Hill College while Chase tied up the loose ends of an unfinished court case in Asheville. The drive was pleasant enough but the murder of Becky Paul weighed heavily even in this picturesque high country. I'd seen the crime scene photos and the incalculable brutality. Brute force. Hate. Rage. The kind of brutality often seen in crimes of passion. Haze DeBrew moved to the top of my list of suspects. He also had ties to John Roman.

I saw the college sign and exited in its direction. Many red brick buildings greeted me and I had to strain to read the building names as I looked for Cypress Hall, where Steve Paul said Becky attended class. I circled the parking lot three times before finding a space large enough for the Hummer. I eased between two Volkswagens, one with a tattered convertible top.

Skipping up the few cement steps, I entered Cypress Hall and headed for the directory of offices. I found the professor's name on the board: *Aba Finch, Professor of Sociology. Second Floor. Room 45.*

I climbed the stairs and worked my way around several students waiting for class or lining up some plans for later. I found Room 45 empty. Two small desks and chairs were crammed into the office about the size of a closet.

How dismal.

I sighed and began to walk down the hall to have a look around.

"Can I help you?" came a voice from behind me. I faced a woman with white hair and horn-rimmed glasses, a typical professor.

"Yes, ma'am. I'm trying to locate Professor Aba Finch. She isn't in her office."

"I'm Aba Finch. Are you a student of mine? I don't recognize you and I don't remember any young lady quite so tall."

"No, I'm not a student. Could we talk in your office?"

She motioned me in. "You'll have to sit in Professor D'Angelo's chair. She's in class. I'm afraid we don't have much room for conferencing." She sat and straightened her outdated dung brown skirt. "How can I help you?"

I flipped out my badge. "Agent Hunter, ma'am. SBI."

"Oh, my. You must be here because of Ms. Paul. I just heard about it this morning."

"Yes, ma'am. She died on the way home from your class. I need to ask you some questions and I'll need a list of everyone in your class."

"I'll try to help, Agent, but you don't think one of my students killed another, do you?"

"We have to investigate every possibility, Professor. Was Becky Paul in class last week?"

"Yes, but a few minutes tardy. She seemed embarrassed to walk in late, but I'm sure she had a good reason. She's never tardy. I can't say the same for many of the other younger students. Ms. Paul was a little older and more mature, don't you know? The reason I remember her tardiness is because she's never been tardy."

"Did she seem upset? Anxious? Any reason to think something bothered her?"

"Well, no, except for being tardy. Of course, I lectured, so I kept on with my lesson. She just took a seat and got out her notebook, don't you know?" Her lips were encircled with deep wrinkles.

"Any friends she hangs with during breaks or after class?"

"I've never really seen her with anyone, although I take a break myself. Students have time to go to the snack machines and restrooms. I've talked to her enough to know she's married and has two children, girls, I think. She'd get right up from the desk and head out the door once I dismissed class. I don't think she did much socializing with the other students unless during our twenty-minute break. Like I said, there's a considerable age difference—probably every bit of fifteen to twenty years older than most of the students in the class. And she had a long drive at night. That's the only complaint I've heard from her; she'd be glad when the drive ended, don't you know?"

"So you don't think anybody here can tell me anything about her? Her habits, nothing?"

"Agent Hunter, I hate to frustrate you but Becky stayed to herself, came for class, and left campus. I don't know what else to tell you. I'm sorry. She was a nice person, I believe. I can't imagine why anyone would want to hurt her." I got Professor Aba's list of students and headed for the parking lot.

"Excuse me."

I watched as a petite blonde approached. "I'm Marie Downey. Becky was in my class." A name in Becky's phone book. She had my attention. "Do you have time for a cup of coffee?"

"Sure." I introduced myself as we walked to the commons area. I ordered a chai tea latte and she got a cappuccino. We sat at a bistro table.

"I figured someone would come to question us since she died on the way home from class."

"We're trying to contact anyone who might know what happened, her state of mind, who she hangs with here."

"I'm the only one. I mean, Becky was friendly but most of these students are kids, late teens, early twenties. I'm twenty-seven, married with two children. I guess we had more in common. We had casual conversations at the snack machines and a couple of times we came over here and got something hot to drink. She told me she was married with two daughters. She'd also told me she was getting some cosmetic work done soon. She wasn't satisfied with her looks."

"Ms. Downey, did she ever mention trouble in her marriage or anybody bothering her? Was she afraid of anyone?"

"She seemed happy. She bragged about her husband all the time. She never mentioned being troubled. Why? Did her husband kill her?"

"Oh, no, no. We just have to ask those questions. Please don't read anything into what I'm asking. I just have to cover every possible angle. On the last night you saw her, I understand she came in late."

"Yeah, I could tell she was uncomfortable about that. At break she said she had a conference with an irate parent after school and had a difficult time leaving to get to class. She also said she dreaded the drive home in the fog. She hadn't eaten anything either. I offered her some Nabs but she said she'd pick up something hot after class."

"I don't suppose she named the angry parent?"

"No, sorry."

"Did you ever see her talking with other students who might help me?"

"No. Like I said, she was friendly enough to say 'Hello' and 'See you later', but I think I'm the only one she really had a conversation with."

I thanked Marie Downey and tossed my empty cup in the trash.

I drove the desolate road to the crime scene, stopped, and got out where a dark stain still covered the narrow right lane and what little shoulder existed. Its edges had been combed hurriedly so the road could reopen. This road had no turnarounds—one way here and one way out. The parkway couldn't afford to close it for a lengthy investigation.

Chase bagged some blood, took a few pictures, and quickly swabbed the car for prints or trace that could answer some questions. It was possible on that dark, foggy night trace had been overlooked. I stood still as much out of respect as frustration.

I went over every square inch of the road and shoulders, snapping pictures with my PDA. I climbed over a piece of rusty rail just far enough to see I couldn't walk on that side without endangering my life. Clinging to the rail I pulled myself back onto the road, leaning back over far enough to observe thick kudzu webbed as far as I could see. I snapped a few pictures. I could always delete them later.

The view is breath taking.

A lump caught in my throat, standing in the space where Becky Paul drew her last breath. No birds sang. No frogs from Banjo Creek croaked. No breeze dared to stir.

•

You pissed in the bed again? What ails you? Pull them sheets off so's I can rub 'em in your face. What you's doin' in thar? Feelin' yourself up? Ain't I enough for ya?

14

I picked the next teachers' workday to go back to Dulcimer High School. After checking in with Dr. Zack, I got a map and headed for individual classrooms, hoping to speak to a few teachers alone. My first stop: Ms. Butter, in Family and Consumer Science. Her first name was Marjorie but she quickly confessed that students called her "Margarine" behind her back. We both laughed.

"I guess you're here about John Roman."

"Yes. I see you were on a first-name basis with him."

"Most of us were, actually. He told me to call him John instead of Mr. Roman."

"What kind of relationship did you have with him?"

She looked at me over her glasses. "I'm a teacher; he's a janitor. What do you mean by 'relationship'?" She seemed offended. "I didn't have a relationship with that man!"

"I meant how did you and Mr. Roman interact here at school, Mrs. Butter. I've been told he sometimes took administrative matters into his own hands, you know, trying to help Dr. Zack out."

"He didn't do anything out of line, as far as I know. He did sometimes snatch boys out of the bathroom who were smoking and haul them down to the office. But we were all supposed to monitor the halls and bathrooms, not just our classrooms. I don't see anything wrong with that."

"No, that's a great help, of course. But how did the students take it? Did he have enemies among the students?"

"Not that I'm aware. They ridiculed him sometimes and called him by his first name. I corrected them, because I can't stand disrespect. It didn't seem to bother John that much though."

"How often did he clean your room?"

"Twice a week usually. That's the thing I got upset about. He'd sometimes make comments about how dirty the room had gotten since he last swept in here. But you have to realize I have large classes and they don't always wipe their feet. One day not long after I came here, he said I was too messy. That really hurt my feelings, but some of the other teachers said he'd told them the same thing, not to worry about it. I let it go."

She walked over to me. "Agent Hunter, I liked John and as far as I know he liked me, professionally. And that's all I know." I thanked her and she directed me to the next teacher on my list.

I found Ms. Barbee. Not a blonde and certainly not built like a Barbie doll. Although young, she had to weigh over two hundred pounds. I introduced myself and asked the same questions I'd asked Ms. Butter.

"I never had any problems with Mr. Roman other than the time he told me I needed to get organized. It made me mad to begin with, until I realized he was right. He couldn't even sweep well because I had piles of stuff on the floor. I stayed late one Monday afternoon and got it all off the floor. He came in to sweep on Tuesday and said he was proud of me.

"Agent Hunter, I don't know why anyone would hurt that man. He talked to me about his wife occasionally. He was so good to her. I know she misses him terribly. He must have been a good cook. He sometimes shared a recipe with me." I thanked her and got directions to the third teacher on my list.

She could have been a Barbie doll. Laurel Philpott, English teacher. Young, blonde, with sizable boobs and a tiny waist.

"Dr. Zack said you'd probably talk to me, Agent Hunter."

"That's why I'm here. Did you get along with John Roman?"

"Yes. A real sweetie pie. He brought me brown sugar bars sometimes. They were to die for." She threw her hand over her mouth. "Oh, my God! I didn't mean to say that." She blushed.

"It's okay, Miss Philpott. I understand how you meant it."

"He'd hold doors for the ladies, go and help us retrieve heavy things from our cars, you know, considerate. Thoughtful. In fact, he apologized for the other guy once. He was my protector, I suppose. Sometimes even my male students would make offhand remarks. Mr. Roman said it was because I was such a looker. He didn't mean anything but a compliment."

"Who did he apologize for?"

"The other maintenance man who came over from the county office some times to do things Mr. Roman didn't know how to do."

"This other man's name, Miss Philpott?"

"Mr. DeBrew. His first name was Haze, I think. Unusual."

"Haze DeBrew?"

"Yeah. I mean, yes ma'am."

"Why did Mr. Roman need to apologize for Mr. DeBrew?" She had my full attention.

"Mr. DeBrew made suggestive remarks, and not just to me, but sometimes to the students as well. He came in here to fix a light fixture one afternoon while I graded papers at my desk. I went to the office and when I came back he asked my name. I told him 'Miss Philpott' and he said 'I'd sure like to fill your pot.'" I'm sure I turned three shades of red, but I laughed it off, got my purse, and left. I mentioned it to Mr. Roman, not really so he'd say anything to Mr. DeBrew, but just because sometimes Mr. Roman and I talked while he swept up. I mean, I get plenty of lines like that. It'll be a pleasure to marry and change my name some day."

"What Mr. DeBrew did was sexual harassment. Did you report it to Dr. Zack?"

"Not until after Mr. DeBrew got fired for peeping at girls. I guess I should have, but I figured he meant it as a compliment. It never occurred to me he might be a pervert, and he wasn't bad looking. Just not my type."

"What did Dr. Zack say about it?"

"She just said the problem had been resolved."

15

The rain, a frog strangler, and not needed after all we'd had the past four days, continued anyway. The Hummer climbed the curvy mountain road with Chase right behind me in his Jeep. We'd decided to interrogate Haze DeBrew with some specific questions. After that I planned to head in another direction while Chase would return to the office. I rose into the higher elevations on the narrow switchback. I blinked at something moving on the road ahead: an escalator of mud rolling at high speed.

I threw the Hummer in reverse with nowhere to go, Chase right behind me, and no time to warn him. I gripped the steering wheel and held on as the mudslide hit hard, relieved mountains were on both sides, and the limbs in the slide seemed small. I glanced in my rearview as the Jeep slid into the right embankment with a loud bang. The Hummer sat still, I guess because of its higher, wider chassis. After a few minutes the worst was past us and I hopped out to check on Chase.

"Are you all right? I didn't have time to warn you."

"Yeah, but Logan, that's probably just the beginning. We've gotta get outta here!" He abandoned his Jeep and jumped into the Hummer as another gush rounded the bend, this time bringing trees and boulders with it. I swung around and headed for higher ground at a high rate of speed. Unable to reach DeBrew's house to ask questions, we headed back to the sheriff's department to go over the evidence and notes we'd collected so far, and to call in Chase's Jeep casualty.

Later in the day I drove Chase to Asheville to pick up a rental car until he could decide his transportation issue. On the way back, I went to Grange Elementary School to find out the name of Becky's angry parent and how to reach him.

The school buses had just left with the children when I entered the office. The school's receptionist instantly gave me a name.

"That'd be Woodrow Teed. He's..." she looked around to see if anyone had come into the office, "...he's not only a Combo Butt but also an asshole."

I laughed. "Tell me how you really feel."

"Agent Hunter, no one can stand him. He's a pompous ass with a prissy boy he thinks is the next Mozart. Irving. Becky has come early, stayed late, and even had lessons outside of school to try to help the kid improve. But you can't make stew beef without meat, you know what I mean?" I nodded. "She usually taught him in the afternoons since Carrie came before school several times a week."

"Who's Carrie?"

"She's a student here. She's in the sixth grade. She's talented. Becky thought she was worth helping. Carrie's very upset about Becky's death."

I made a note. "Have you got the demographics so I can reach Mr. Teed?"

She printed out the information for me with his business phone and address. "He's a lawyer in Asheville. You can find him downtown. It's an older brick building near Fuddrucker's."

"What about Carrie? Can I get her last name and demographics, just in case I need to speak with her?"

"Sure. As a matter of fact, her dad came by here one day right after Becky died and said Carrie'd mentioned some man coming to the classroom. Carrie said it upset Becky."

"Would that have been Mr. Teed?"

"I don't think so. Mr. Teed stayed up here in the office and laid into Becky when she came to her office box. He wanted to create a scene. He always creates a scene."

"Do you have any idea who might have gone to her room?"

"No. Everybody is supposed to check in here, but they don't always follow the rules."

I got information on both students and how to reach the parents, thanked her, and made some phone calls.

~~~~~

Mr. Teed wasn't in court so I headed back into Asheville. He greeted me as I entered his office.

"Agent Hunter?"

I shook his hand, flashed my badge, and followed him to his office, wondering how he could even waddle. He had the biggest butt wagon I'd ever seen. He flopped into a worn high-back executive chair. I could swear I heard the springs whine. I took a less worn leather chair in front of him.

"I heard about Mrs. Paul. I can't believe anyone would hurt such a sweetheart. She taught my Irving piano. I really didn't expect to be interrogated though."

"Sir, it seems you visited her at school the day she died."

"Uh, I fail to see what that has to do with her death."

"My understanding is your conference made her late for her graduate class at Mars Hill, and she had to walk in late and distraught. I need to know what the conference involved."

"Irving and lessons, the same as always. You see, I encouraged her to push Irving. He's lazy. I met with her frequently, but I didn't realize I caused her to be late for a class. She never mentioned it."

"Did you have an appointment with her?"

"No. I just showed up. She's never complained about that either."

"Did you discuss anything that would have left her upset, Mr. Teed?"

He fumbled around the edge of his desk. "Maybe."

"Maybe? Can you elaborate?"

"I wasn't happy with the progress, or should I say lack of progress, Irving made. He should improve at some point, you know? I may have raised my voice a bit. I can sometimes get loud. I just wanted her to light a fire under him, get him moving along. It's expensive, you know." I didn't. "I told her I might look for someone else since she couldn't get the job done. I shouldn't have said that. She's the best around."

"Did you threaten her?"

"No. No, Agent Hunter. I wouldn't. I know better. I kinda stormed out though. I owe her an apology. I just want my son to play beautifully."

"Is that what he wants?" I just couldn't help myself.

"Your time is up, Agent Hunter." He stood and waddled around the desk to show me out.

He should change his name to Mr. Turd.

"Am I a suspect in her murder?"

"Everybody's a suspect at this time, sir. Have a nice day." I'm sure I smirked. I couldn't help but enjoy making him uncomfortable.

~~~~~

Carrie Georgiadis was twelve-years-old and I knew better than to interrogate her without a parent's permission. Her father, a pharmacist at the only non-private drugstore in Madison County, bobbed up and down behind the counter, pouring pills into bottles. I had to wait about thirty minutes for him to fill prescriptions for waiting customers. Once the crowd dissipated, he asked me to step behind the counter and go into a small office where we could talk.

"Agent Hunter, I'm Anthony Geordiadis, as I guess you already know."

"Yes, sir. I'm here because the school receptionist said you'd made a comment about Carrie and Becky Paul."

"Yes. Becky's been giving piano lessons to Carrie for four years. I'd drop her off in the mornings on my way here and Becky was wonderful enough to go in early. She said Carrie showed promise. She's been in three recitals, each one more difficult than the previous one."

"I understand Carrie told you Ms. Paul seemed upset the day she died."

"Carrie came home that afternoon and I asked her about her day, as usual. She said everything was fine but she didn't accomplish much during her music lesson. I asked why. She said when she got to the classroom a man stood in the doorway talking to Becky. Carrie said Becky told him to leave."

"Did he?"

"Yes, but he told Becky he'd be back."

"Why did that seem odd to Carrie?"

"She's twelve. I don't think she'd have thought it odd except Becky acted nervous and anxious during the lesson. She apologized to Carrie and said she'd be fine. Late that night I heard about Becky on the scanner. At first I thought it was a wreck. Then I heard what really happened. I was so shocked that someone could beat her like that. A sweet person, Agent Hunter, and no one deserves that."

"Did Carrie have any idea who the man was?"

"Becky's ex-husband, DeBrew. She said she'd seen him talking to Becky before. I've always heard he was a talented carpenter but a hot head. You're welcomed to talk with Carrie if you need to."

I thanked Mr. Geordiadis and left.

16

I could hear a sound to the left of DeBrew's house, but couldn't determine where it came from as Chase rang the bell. Maybe a stream or rapids. Chase told me this was waterfall country, part of the Pisgah National Forest.

"Good morning, Mr. DeBrew. I'm Logan Hunter, SBI, and I believe you know Detective Railey," I said to the man who opened the door and looked at my badge. He seemed stunned and somewhat upset to see us.

"Haze, we need to ask you a few questions about Becky," Chase said.

DeBrew opened the door and we walked into the house he'd built himself. We stood in the living room. A large fireplace made of small boulders from the mountains themselves made it spectacular, with the huge cedar beams running above and below it. Some of the light fixtures were hung at the top of the beams on the vaulted ceiling, not an easy task.

"I told you he was a great carpenter and electrician," Chase said to me before turning toward DeBrew. "I'd informed Agent Hunter you do most of the handy work in the high country and people just keep coming back to you. I've never been here before. It's awesome!" Chase exclaimed.

DeBrew rubbed his peculiarly red eyes. "Thank you. Now, how can I help you? I need to get some work done so I can go to Becky's memorial service." His eyes were such a light blue they appeared to be almost transparent inside the red sockets—not easy to look at—and one tooth near the corner of his mouth looked somewhat like a short fang. I shook the thoughts out of my head.

"Mr. DeBrew, where were you the Tuesday night Becky Paul died?" I asked, looking straight at him.

"In Tennessee, near Newport, finishing a job," he replied. I noticed his bandaged hand. My pulse raced.

"What happened to your hand?" I had my PDA ready for his response, making a specific note his knuckles were bandaged.

He pulled up his injured hand, studying it himself. "Stupidity. I hurt myself on the last day of a job in Tennessee. I was there three days. I can show you hotel bills, and the doctor's bill if you want to see it." He walked to a desk to retrieve the note. "Something distracted me and I hit my knuckles with my claw hammer. I fractured several. It's painful," he explained in his baritone voice.

"I'm sure it is. Mr. DeBrew, what kind of relationship did you and your ex-wife have? Did you ever run into her?"

"You don't waste any time, do you? We had a great relationship. I never blamed her for leaving me. I used to drink a lot. The split wasn't good at first, but over the years, we became friends again. I used to think we might get back together. I saw her not long before this happened. She seemed happy. She has two daughters, you know. Not mine, but sweet girls—like their mother." He handed me the doctor's note from Medic-Quik in Newport. I made the notation in my Palm Pilot.

"Are you aware of any enemies she might have?"

"Becky? No, she wouldn't have any enemies. Agent Hunter. As sweet as anybody I've ever met. Genuine. Sincere. No, she didn't have enemies. This had to be some kind of accident."

"Believe me, it was no accident," Chase said.

He walked us to the door and we told him not to go out of town; we might have more questions.

"I don't plan on going anywhere. I hope you can get the bastard who did this to Becky. I still loved her." Haze's voice quivered. "Now if you'll excuse me, I have to get ready."

"One second, Mr. DeBrew. Did you know John Roman?"

"I'm sure you already know I knew him, Agent. We worked together."

"That's right. Did you and Mr. Roman get along?"

"Yes. Well, in fact. John cleaned floors and stuff like that as good as anybody I know, but he'd call me if something broke or had to be built. The school system doesn't have much money, so we saved a lot by doing it ourselves."

"Did Mr. Roman help you with projects?"

"Sometimes, but usually he didn't know how and would have been in the way. We ate dinner together a lot, though. Over at Dulcimer. Ask anyone."

"Did he ever mention any enemies?"

"No." DeBrew seemed sincere. We were getting nowhere on either case.

It had taken so long to get to DeBrew's that Chase needed to get home and change for the memorial service. Since the service was near Taryn's house, I had enough time to dress.

•

So you wanna fight me, do ya? You think your man enough to take me on? Well, let's see whatcha got, wimp, pussy, maggot…

•

The memorial service, set for late afternoon so school employees, as well as students and parents, could attend together, started with soft music. The largest church in the community was packed. The flower arrangements touched the walls on both sides. Four large palms snuggled between handled baskets of carnations, daisies, roses, lilies, and baby's breath. The music continued and mingled with the congregation's sobs and sniffles as we entered the church.

I recognized Mr. Geordiadis in the front pew, beside a small girl, apparently his daughter Carrie. She rose and moved to the piano, playing the sweet sound of "Fairest Lord Jesus" recognizable to all of us. She did have promise.

I scanned the congregation to see if I knew anyone other than Steve. He had a young girl hugged up close on each side of him. Other family members sat farther down the same bench. Chase punched me and I looked in his direction, spotting Haze DeBrew, with handkerchief out, already wiping tears.

The service consisted of two eulogies, one from Becky Paul's principal, the other from her dear friend and colleague Peggy Hoilman. Chase and I eased out slowly with the rest of the crowd once the family cleared the church steps. By the time we reached the exterior doors, the limo drove away with the family. We headed toward the parking lot and again saw Haze DeBrew, sobbing, with several ladies around to comfort him. Apparently even though they divorced, he still loved Becky.

•

Quit your cryin'. You'd think I's hittin' you instead of your maw. You'll get what's comin' to you later on.

17

After getting the tour of Chase's new red Jeep Wrangler Rubicon, we dug into a platter of French toast smothered with butter and blueberry syrup. Raina wasn't working, so Gertie Myers waited on us, but quiet and engaged every second, her attention wasn't solely focused on us. When she had a chance, she brought us extra bacon and plenty of coffee. The place was busier than usual with some folks I'd never noticed before.

I saw the huge man when he entered the grill, every bit of six feet five, built like a lumberjack. His ink black hair and sharp nose identified him as Cherokee. He looked around for a few seconds and made a beeline in our direction. Chase's back was to the man I thought was passing our table, but instead he stopped right beside our booth and faced us.

Chase swallowed his toast, saw the man, and turned white. A muscular arm reached out and snatched Chase out from under the table. All activity stopped; all eyes were on Big Thug.

"What's the deal, DeWayne? What's your problem?"

"You, R..Railey. You b..better stay away from R..Raina or I'll t..tear off your limbs and feed'em to my hawgs," came the growling response.

"I haven't touched Raina. We're history. We have been for a long time." Everyone had put forks down, and this DeWayne had the stage.

"N..Not what I'm gettin' from her." He popped an unexpecting Chase hard in the nose, creating instant blood. He turned him loose and let him fall hard into his seat. I reached for the gun in my ankle pocket as the man lumbered toward the door, yelling back, "Just a p..preview of things to come." I stood to go after him, but Chase's hand came out to restrain me.

"Let it go, Logan. I'll take this up with Raina." I dropped back into my seat as Gertie handed Chase a wet kitchen towel to stop the bleeding.

"Chase, that man assaulted you."

"No joke."

"Aren't you going to do something?"

A voice from behind me yelled, "Hey, Railey, you gonna let Lamplighter get away with that? You got guns. Go get him!"

Chase wiped his nose and said nothing. We'd both lost our appetites and I walked out behind Chase. I had to admit he'd stayed calm. He hadn't let his anger show, hadn't raised his voice.

"Let me make something clear. I can fight my own battles, Logan." Chase wiped blood, but his eyes penetrated mine. I wanted to apologize but he cut me off. "Look, I've got some things to take care of. I'll catch up with you later."

"Chase, where are you going?"

He didn't answer, and I didn't say anything more. I just hoped he wouldn't do anything foolish as I watched him hop into the shiny new Rubicon and spit rocks.

18

Logan, I'm glad you're home early. Come and meet Ceil," Taryn called from the kitchen. I entered to see a beaming bottled blonde grinning at me.

"Logan, this is Cecilia Nesbitt, my pal."

"Hello, Ms. Nesbitt. I've heard about you. I think it's great you ladies live close enough to enjoy each other."

"I've heard so much about you, Agent Hunter. Taryn is thrilled to have an SBI agent staying here. She thinks it's so exciting. But please call me Cecilia or Ceil."

"If you'll call me Logan. I understand you sing. I hope I get a chance to hear you."

"Come to church Sunday, Logan. She's singing two solos at our little church just down the road," Taryn said. I told them I'd try. "Now, I myself can't carry a tune in the back of my Pathfinder." We all laughed.

"My son Roy told me about your Hummer. He thinks it's the best thing since hot apple jacks."

"I met him at the Sheriff's office. Chase Railey introduced us."

"That Chase is a good-looking somebody, isn't he? You two would make a nice couple."

I'm sure I blushed.

"Well, come on, Ceil. If we're going to paint that quilt block, we better get started," Taryn said.

"Oh, Taryn, I've been meaning to ask you about those. I see them on barns all over the place. How many have you done?"

"Ceil and I have only painted two. I'm usually working on the real deals because tourists like to buy Appalachian bed quilts. A woman from Ohio started the signs tradition and our artists and quilters picked up on the idea to help preserve our quilting heritage. The blocks are now in at least six western counties in the state. It's called a Quilt Trail. Some businesses have gotten behind the project and donated the metal signs and paint. It's become a community thing. I know Boone and West Jefferson have some. I expect you'll see more and more of them going up on barns."

"I'm not much of an artist, but I can paint the signs if Taryn makes the lines. All I have to do is get the right color in each one," Ceil added. "I like to see them around too. Makes me proud to be part of the project."

"I love the idea. I'll keep my eyes open for more of them, and you should both be proud to live here and be a part of such a great idea."

~~~~~

Sunday came and I pulled out the one skirt I'd brought with me. I didn't like to wear dresses or skirts, but sometimes I found it unavoidable. While some women were comfortable wearing pants to church, I wasn't raised that way and felt compelled to put on the black skirt and look for a top.

"You don't have a single frock?" I shook my head as Taryn scrambled through an array of tops I'd laid across my bed. "Well, any of them will go with black but I like the turquoise." She disappeared and returned with a gorgeous handmade silver necklace and earrings she insisted I wear. I really felt dressed up because the jewelry perfectly accentuated the plain turquoise top.

The Luck Primitive Baptist Church was close enough to walk if it weren't for the treacherous road we'd have to walk on, so Taryn drove. The small white board church— freshly painted—looked in good shape, especially considering it was over one hundred and fifty years old. We walked up the front steps and into the main doors. We both signed a huge book just inside the vestibule. We had a choice of going into the congregational area through left or right doors. I noticed other doors but had no idea where they went.

"My daddy always said 'Go right and you can't go wrong,'" I whispered to Taryn as I followed her to the right. Long pews lined the center of the church with shorter rows on each side. Many of them held personal pillows, perhaps to mark the territory as well as to comfort a weak back during a long sermon. A balcony on both sides solved the other door mystery. At the front a pulpit with steep steps on either side caught my attention. We neared the front pew before I saw the preacher on a posh velvet settee behind it. It looked far more comfortable than the stiff, high-backed chairs I remembered from the Southern Baptist church of my childhood.

Ceil appeared and waved as she sat down by the organist. While I wasn't comfortable in the front pew, Taryn insisted on showing me off. I decided not to protest. The small church filled with people behind us, but I didn't turn. A few fingers tapped Taryn's shoulders and folks whispered until the preacher stood and gave the signal for all of us to rise.

We read several scripture passages with him and once we settled in our seats once more, Cecilia Nesbitt stood. Taryn punched me to make certain I knew she was going to sing. I recognized the tune. Cecilia sang "No One Ever Cared for Me Like Jesus". It had been a while since I'd been to church but I was pleased to be in this tiny church in the dale listening to one of the most angelic voices I'd ever heard.

I sat motionless and nodded at Cecilia once she finished. I listened intently to the preacher's message about how we needed to care more about each other. He briefly mentioned the murders. His prayer included God giving guidance and strength to those who sought evil and plucked it out—music to my ears. It validated what I did and why I did it.

Cecilia stood again, and I literally broke out in goose bumps as she sang "Amazing Grace." We hung around after church to wait for Cecilia to join us for dinner. Taryn introduced me to the preacher and a few folks in the congregation. Glad I'd come to the church service, I looked forward with growing anticipation to the fried chicken Taryn cooked that morning.

•

Hadn't I tol you to stop pissin' in the bed? I swear thar's somethin' wrong with you, boy.

19

Three weeks later

Joyce Beech had been home about an hour, just long enough to fry some pork chops and green tomatoes he could recognize by peeping through her French door screens. He watched through the double-screened doors as she boiled a couple of ears of corn she'd apparently frozen last summer. She disappeared long enough to slip into a housecoat and Sponge Bob slippers, most likely given to her by one of her middle school students.

~~~~~

He could see several stacks of papers on the desk as he peeked in. He didn't doubt she was a good math teacher, preparing student for the state's required End-Of-Grade tests, and always getting high scores. He'd been in her classroom a time or two and the kids loved her and worked their math problems while she guided them. He'd seen her outside with them, making the beautiful mountain setting fit into her math lessons somehow. He liked that much about her. Even if she was black.

She was young—he'd guess about twenty-seven—and seemed hell bent to stay in Madison County to teach. He couldn't blame her, but she was out of her element. Being a black female teacher here made her a conspicuous minority. And he had no use for uppity Yankees, whatever color.

It surprised him that a Chicago inner-city black girl wanted a forty-five-minute drive one way each day to school, but she evidently liked living out away from other folks, as he did. At least they had that in common. Her house was nice, and when she needed repairs, she called him. That's where the trouble started. She owed him for the carpentry work he'd done a few months back. He'd torn out and completely redesigned her bathroom, transforming it from ordinary into spa—expensive, but she'd paid over half when he finished the job, promising the rest on her next payday. He'd sent her several bills, the last one with a hostile note, but she always giggled and apologized, laying it off to procrastination. Still she hadn't paid up.

He could see Joyce pouring herself a glass of cheap wine and sitting down to enjoy her pork chops and tomatoes. He'd let her enjoy her meal.

She finished her second chop while put his plan into effect. A sound like a motor filled the night air for a second, reminding him animals frequented the valley fields, making unusual noises, especially during mating season. She didn't come out.

He could see a few deer grazing under her apple trees. He enjoyed their peaceful presence as he gave her time to finish her food and drop her dish and fork in the sink. He watched as she walked to the back door and peered into the night, opened the screen door and walked into the backyard a few yards from the house. She bent over, picked up a limb from one of the trees, and took a deep breath of mountain air, looking up at a sky filled with glitter.

As the gnawing sound filled the night, she turned toward him and then raced toward the house. He ran at her full speed with the sharpened chain saw, its ugly loud teeth grinding close to her. She jumped and yelped, but not quick enough to avoid the first cut which took away her right forearm. Blood gushed from her stunned body as she ran, screaming, toward the house. He jumped in front of her, blocking her escape. She lost blood fast but still tried to dodge around the side of the house toward her Four Runner, wrapping her stump in the bottom of her nightgown. Her bedroom slippers made her stumble and she fell to the ground, looking up at him with terror-filled eyes. She seemed to realize she wasn't going to escape the swish of the saw that would lop off her head.

Frenzy! Exhilaration! Satisfaction. He was covered with blood. Hell, the whole world was covered with blood. Body parts lay in inelegant positions all around the backyard once he'd completed his deed. What a thrill to see the terror in her eyes as he zipped the saw through her neck and watched the head topple off. What a rush to swish away arms and legs, leaving nothing but a bloody torso!

He went inside and took a long hot shower in Joyce's new tub, gratifying his aroused groin before reaching down and scooping a few pubic hairs from the tub drain and spraying some convenient antibacterial foaming cleaner to erase any semen or blood. He took his bloody clothes, the towel, the cloth, and the shoes, and tossed them into a trash bag he'd take with him. He ran to the kitchen and grabbed the Clorox. He knew that would kill his DNA. He poured most of the contents in the tub and trickled remnants over his tracks as he backed out of the house.

Always prepared, he'd worn clothes and shoes he didn't intend to wear again so all he had to do was burn the evidence. Bloody footprints might lead into the house, but they didn't lead out. They'd go unnoticed since he'd smeared the thick blood everywhere. He wondered if Tall Skinny Bitch in a Hummer could figure this one out.

He smoked a cigarette on the way back to his place, not far away. This kill had been especially enjoyable. Better than any sex he'd ever had. He didn't dislike Joyce Beech, but damn it, she wouldn't pay up. He reminded himself he needed to mark her account "Paid in Full" when he got home, in case Tall Skinny Bitch asked questions.

He pulled over on a deserted road just before the state line. He took his bag of blood-soaked items and walked to a roadside grill beside a picnic table. He tossed the lump into the grill, poured on a little gas and ignited it. Even if someone rode by, they'd just think he was grilling.

It took a few minutes to burn the evidence before he turning his truck around and headed home. He went around several high narrow roads with no metal barriers. He laughed like a maniac and couldn't stop. He envisioned just driving right off the side of the high mountain, becoming a ball of flame, putting an end to all of it. But he couldn't make himself do it. Was he enjoying it too much, or was he just a coward? Shaking, he turned into the dirt path to his isolated house.

He took his bagged souvenir out to the freezer and dropped it in. Walking to his bathroom closet, he added the letter "C" to the inside of the door with his marker before drinking a pint of Jose Cuervo straight from the bottle.

20

Tired when I got home, I barely noticed the car beside Taryn's Pathfinder. I headed for my bedroom with a few new clothes I'd bought in Asheville, including a new nightgown and slippers and one navy frock. Taryn would be pleased about the frock. I tossed the bag on my bed and stretched out beside it, closing my eyes for a few minutes. I'm not sure if I went to sleep. I could hear noises but I couldn't seem to get my eyes open or to decipher what the noises were. I heard loud gasps coming from Taryn's bedroom, sat up, and listened carefully.

Is she in trouble?

I dashed around the corner and opened the door, thinking maybe she was having a heart attack.

"Taryn, are you all...er...OH MY GOD!" I stood frozen, my eyes locked on the foot-long neon green dildo strapped around a naked Cecilia Nesbitt.

"Oh, my God!" Taryn tried to cover up, but not before I saw the butterfly tattoo on her hefty buttocks.

I somehow closed the door, hearing myself whisper "Sorry." I unclawed my hand from the doorknob and raced to my room.

My God! Taryn's a lesbian! Green dildo. Neon. Oh my God!

I grabbed my Hummer keys from under shopping bags just as Taryn came in with her robe on.

"Logan…"

"I'm sorry, Taryn. I should've knocked. I'm so sorry."

"What must you think of me, Logan? I should've told you. Let me explain. I…." She noticed I held keys in my hand. "I hope you're not leaving."

"Yes. Yes, I am. I need to leave. I think I need to give you privacy. I'll go into town or over to the grill for awhile."

"No, please don't. We need to talk about this."

"It's none of my business, Taryn. This is your house and you're a grown woman. I shouldn't have barged in. It's just that I thought you were in pain. It never occurred to me that you were…uh…well, you know."

The door creaked open and Cecilia came in—minus the dildo.

"There's fresh coffee. Why don't the three of us have some and I'll go home."

Awkwardly we all walked to the kitchen and poured mugs. Taryn pulled out some bourbon and poured a little in hers. I extended my mug for the same. I wanted the floor to cave in and remove me from this situation. We headed to the porch, the neon dildo still foremost in my mind.

Once we all took a few swigs of spiked coffee, Cecilia initiated the conversation. Taryn and I didn't make eye contact, both too embarrassed.

"Taryn thinks you're pretty open-minded," Cecilia began. "Is that so?"

I looked at each of them, both without husbands, middle-aged and probably lonely. "I'd like to think I am." I fidgeted in my seat and spilled some of my coffee. I mopped with my napkin and took a big gulp of my beverage. The warm bourbon coffee would calm my nerves. Maybe. I still hadn't made eye contact with either of them.

Taryn perched on a stool she'd painted and leaned back with her coffee, barely touching the porch screen. She made eye contact with me but apparently leaned too far, sending her ample body through the old screen and tearing a sizable gap in it. I gawked as her legs and behind flipped into the flowerbed outside. Cecilia and I ran to the damaged screen and peered at Taryn.

"Are you hurt?" I didn't know whether to laugh or cry.

Taryn, covered with coffee and embarrassment, hopped up before I could get outside to lift her. "I'm fine, damn it. Ceil, I want straight whiskey!"

Ceil raced to the kitchen while I waited for Taryn to limp gingerly back to the porch. I remained silent.

After we were all situated again, the ladies, mostly Cecilia, talked while I guzzled, trying to take in how they accidentally found each other and something in themselves they never knew existed. Neither tried to seduce the other; it just happened, over years of comfortable, trusting friendship. Two intelligent and talented ladies, not doing anyone any harm and enjoying each other, keeping loneliness at bay. I nodded some degree of understanding as they talked on, wanting me to be comfortable with the situation. They loved each other, but I knew it would take a while for me to adjust to this latest surprise.

21

Chase and I met for breakfast again at the Trust Grill. We'd eaten there so much we had our own designated booth. I hadn't slept, keeping one eye open all night. I guess I trusted Taryn, but. I was just shaken. I decided not to tell Chase about my latest discovery, a private matter between Taryn, Cecilia, and me. We had to concentrate on more deadly situations anyway. Every suspect had been frustrating so far. I ordered an omelet and Chase got a stack of hotcakes that looked scrumptious.

"How about a bite?"

He cut a thick section and put his fork over to my mouth and I leisurely sucked them in with

My eyes closed. *This is our first intimate moment.* When I opened my eyes, he smiled as though he read my mind. I felt my face flush.

"The next time I have breakfast here, it's hotcakes with warm syrup. They're magnificent!" I called out to Otis Frye, the cook. I finished my coffee and pulled out my notes. "By the way, did you get things straight with Mr. Lamplighter?"

"Probably not. I talked to Raina. She admitted she'd told him to take a hike. She actually had delusions about us getting back together. We dated for over three years, but she wanted to get married. I'm not ready for that, and, for the record, I'm not in love with her."

"She's beautiful."

"Yeah, but, clingy like honeysuckle vines. Or kudzu." We laughed. "I tried to find DeWayne but it's probably best I didn't. Some of his folks are mean. I can't say I blame them. The Cherokee weren't treated well, if you remember your history. He's part of the Wild Potato clan."

"I thought I knew my history, but you've lost me with the potato thing."

"The Cherokee Nation has seven clans. They first came to the Smoky Mountains over a thousand years ago, believing it to be their ancestral home. Marriage was allowed between members of different clans, but not to outsiders like me. Some clans, including DeWayne's clan, still believe in that. Raina, on the other hand, from the Deer clan, changed with modern times, thanks to the considerable efforts of her mother, Calliope. I know you remember the Trail of Tears from your history book." I nodded. "The Cherokee were gathered and forced from their homes. Thousands died. A few hid in these mountains and somehow survived. They're now called The Eastern Band of Cherokee and were allowed to reclaim some of their lands in this area."

Chase's cell phone interrupted us, and when he answered and immediately jumped up, I knew there was another one. We flew out the door and got into the Hummer, Chase briefing me as I backed up.

"A math teacher at County Middle School didn't report for work. The principal sent her assistant and a male teacher to make sure she was all right. Logan, they found her body in her backyard, in pieces, blood everywhere!" Chase nearly screamed at me.

I felt nauseous, taking the mountain curves at a dangerous speed. Joyce Beech lived up in the higher elevations near the Tennessee line. A flock of vultures signaled the location. The air smelled like blood. Too much blood. Human blood. We drove up the gravel path to a ranch-style brick house. Sheriff Yandle, already at the scene, turned as pale as any living human I'd ever seen.

"Railey, Hunter, it's terrible. You can't prepare for what you're about to see," he managed, wiping vomit from his shirt. We walked around to the backyard, saturated with blood. I could see several body parts, unattached from each other. My stomach tried to crawl under my feet to hide. I kept my omelet down with raw determination, and managed to hold it down until I saw her head, some distance away from the other parts. It appeared to have been partially eaten by some animal. I hurled the omelet and coffee.

Sheriff Yandle and other deputies cordoned off the grounds with the familiar bright yellow tape. I had to get a grip. We couldn't have the scene jeopardized. We had to find some evidence to nail this psycho before he struck again.

"Still think these are coincidences, Agent Hunter?" asked the sheriff, wiping his brow.

"No, sir. We're dealing with the same killer. We have our work cut out for us and I promise you we won't stop until we catch this wacko. Each case gets worse. We can't afford to let him strike again." I asked the sheriff to keep everyone away, including the county coroner, until we had time to go over the entire yard. Yandle, now with three knuckles up his butt crack, went inside to look around while Chase and I put on rubber gloves and tried to find all body parts, glad my Palm Pilot was in my pocket. I took pictures and notes as I went, even though they'd be gruesome to study later. It went with the territory.

"Do you see another hand and forearm? I can only find one," a colorless Chase managed to say. We heard a ruckus and turned at the same time. The biggest, most revolting vulture I'd ever seen pecked frantically at the bloody head. I ran toward the bird, screaming at him, and he charged me, flapping his wings and daring me to interfere. I'd never looked a turkey vulture in the eye. He was despicable, and he meant business. He flew at me, squawking, before I could pull my Ruger. I turned to run, but he flapped his wings on my arm and pounced on my chest, clawing my skin as I protected my face. I knocked him off as a shot rang out and the buzzard crumbled at my feet. I trembled for a few minutes while Chase unloaded his rounds into the bird.

"I think he's dead," the sheriff called out from the back door. Chase glowered at Yandle and kicked the buzzard violently before continuing to gather body parts. I stood motionless for a few moments until I calmed a little and Chase moved farther away. I picked up my glasses, bent almost beyond recognition.

Damn shits!

I wiped a few drops of blood off a scratched arm and got back to bits and pieces of the victim.

We bagged the gnarled head, legs, trunk, and the left arm and searched until we were sure the right one could not be found.

"Maybe an animal took it," Chase figured.

"Probably that damned vulture," I responded. I followed the smeared bloody footprints into the back door of the house and suggested Chase look for any vehicle tracks, although gravel didn't generally yield identifiable ones.

Sheriff Yandle walked over to me with a paper. I opened a bill for carpentry work, marked in red, "Third Notice, Pay Up Immediately". I shuddered.

"Haze DeBrew's signature." He was now associated with all three of the victims. I put the bill in a zip-lock bag for evidence.

"He's looking like our best suspect." The sheriff headed for the door. "Oh, and whoever did this poured Clorox all over the floor in the bathroom and out to the door. It'll be nearly impossible to get DNA."

I groaned. Yandle moved toward his car, letting out a seismic fart. I was relieved to be in the open air. He was undoubtedly the crudest man I'd ever met, either scratching his nuts or three knuckles deep up his own ass. Chase joined me at the back door.

"Is the sheriff really as vulgar as he seems?"

"In what way?"

"The farting and scratching his testicles all the time right in front of everybody."

Chase laughed weakly. "All guys fart and scratch their nuts. In Yandle's case though, it's a neuticle."

"Come again?"

"You know, one nut. He had one shot off when he worked the streets of Cincinnati years ago. Haven't you noticed his limp?"

I thought blubber caused that.

"Anyway, don't you dare let him know I told you."

I put my gloved index finger near my lips and handed him the carpentry bill.

"Well, that's interesting. Haze DeBrew again."

"Yeah, but let's not jump the gun quite yet."

I got my evidence kit and went through the house, looking for possible DNA the perp had missed with the Clorox. Even if I found something, it would take weeks to get a report.

22

I drove through Windy Noggin on my way back to Taryn's while Chase headed back to the office with the carpentry bill and swabs and remains I'd bagged and labeled. Taryn decided to cook for Chase and I, and we didn't protest, but none of us could eat the spaghetti sauce. All that red sauce and meat. Ugh! Even the noodles made me nauseous. It really didn't matter what she'd prepared; we were all sickened by the latest crime. I wondered how much more gruesome the killings would become if we didn't capture this madman.

Taryn, antsy about all the victims being from the school system, needed to talk. "Ceil just left. Her son Roy is going to start staying with her at night. We're all so upset about these killings. Someone seems to be targeting us teachers. What do you think it means?" she asked, stirring her spaghetti to death. She noticed that we had not touched ours. "I made a poor choice of food. I'm sorry."

"Taryn, I don't think it would make any difference what you cooked," Chase responded. We didn't know what this latest and most violent crime meant. We didn't know why the killer targeted school personnel yet, but we had to figure this out before someone else died. We moved to the porch table to go over everything we knew. We had to be missing something. I told Chase we had to pay Haze DeBrew another visit.

"We know all three murders have been school employees," I pointed out, using a blank canvas Taryn produced for us. "Let's make a grid of the area." Chase pulled up a chair and took the blue Sharpie I offered. We took a map and charted the location of each murder. I stood back and studied. "Chase, they're all within fifty miles of Trust.

"John Roman, a custodian at Dulcimer High School, Caucasian male, hit with something, and then suffocated—what we call a soft kill. The weapon was a blunt object, maybe a piece of lumber. Then wrapped in thick plastic. No fingerprints. Obviously premeditated to have all these supplies on hand. No evidence left at the scene. Roman's clothes were normal, not bloody, nothing torn. No apparent resistance to the killer, which makes me think he may have been ambushed and had no time to react."

"Or he knew his killer."

"Right. No visible blood other than under his nails where he apparently tried to claw out of the plastic. Killed at his work site. Why there instead of home or somewhere in between? No witnesses, no apparent enemies." Chase and I were both in thought for a moment.

"Then Becky Paul, a music teacher at Grange Elementary. She's a Caucasian female, beaten to death probably with a fist. A hard, violent kill. Her cell phone was on the seat. The only call dialed was to her residence at 9 pm. No call to 9-1-1 or any reason to think she had time to react. She probably died shortly after dialing her home. Did she talk to her husband?"

"No, I think Steve said he and the girls were gone somewhere."

"Blood everywhere but the killer was smart enough to deliberately smear all shoe tracks. No weapon found. Again, no fingerprints. Fibers found in her mouth would indicate a gloved hand beat her. Beaten outside the car and propped up inside. She'd just left class and headed home on an isolated and foggy night. There's no evidence that she fought. Why? Why wouldn't you fight if you knew you were going to die?"

"Maybe she didn't know. Maybe she knew the killer and wasn't afraid." We stared at each other for a second, making mental notes.

"Next is our middle school math teacher, Joyce Beech. She's the only black victim, female. Mutilated. No weapon found. I'd say a chain saw but it hasn't turned up. Hardware stores say every man in the mountains owns at least one. All footprints in and around the house are smeared beyond identification. Blood all over the entire yard and some large smears in the house. I'm thinking the killer finished her off and went inside and took a shower."

"Took a shower, Logan? How do you figure that?"

"He poured Clorox in the tub and on the floors to kill his DNA. Why would he need to do that unless he'd dripped blood into the house?" I turned to face Chase. "He decides to shower to get all the blood off himself. He's smart enough to know he could be leaving behind DNA, so he finds the Clorox."

"That makes sense, but where are his clothes?"

"Didn't the sheriff say there was no towel hanging at the tub? It doesn't prove anything, but my theory is he dried off with Beech's towel, and maybe wrapped it around himself, and took all his bloody clothes with him."

"Pretty good theory, I suppose," Chase said.

"Beech was single and lived in an isolated area, a long way from any other houses. The only document of interest is a bill she owed Haze DeBrew. Judging by the path of blood, I'd guess she was initially attacked near the trees. She ran, injured, toward the house, and maybe decided to head for her car. Maybe she thought she could outrun him. She didn't make it. He finished her off where the majority of the blood is.

"Nothing really ties them together except education. But the killer is smart; he's smearing prints and apparently wearing gloves, and he knows Clorox kills DNA. All murders appear to be premeditated. Why?" I asked.

"But Logan, serial killers historically kill victims of the same sex and same race, and in the same way, don't they?"

"Typically, but this killer isn't fitting the serial pattern, and that makes it tougher on us. We have to develop a profile. We need to profile each victim, more than we've done here, and try to profile the killer. Each murder is more gruesome than the previous one. He knows what he's doing, covering his tracks well, leaving few clues. He's a loner. He may have a stressor causing him to strike certain people, particularly educators. I'm afraid his compulsion to kill is increasing. The question is who fits the profile?" I asked an attentive Chase.

"Haze DeBrew's name keeps coming up. There've got to be some clues here somewhere," he answered, obviously frustrated.

"You're right. DeBrew keeps coming up, but we haven't been able to prove a damn thing, and everything we've uncovered about his relationship with the victims has been sterile. He's got an alibi. He got along with John Roman. They even ate lunch together some times. Even Steve said he still got along too well with Becky. The note he wrote Joyce Beech indicates he's a little pissed with her, but who wouldn't be after months of waiting to be paid for work done?"

Taryn eased out with a tea pitcher and two tall glasses of ice. We thanked her as she disappeared. I'd talked enough to have a parched throat. I guzzled the refreshing tea while I mulled over our conversation so far. I sat my glass down as the ice clanked the sides.

"Let's go back to John Roman. School custodian. Everybody says he's a great guy, nice to everyone, takes care of a sick wife. Looks after the principal. Doesn't seem to have any enemies."

Chase points a finger at me. "But the students. Don't forget he had a problem with some of them."

"Do you really think that little incident would've caused students to kill him? I don't see that, Chase. I don't think those kids did this or know who did."

"For the moment I'm with you. I just want to cover every possibility. We can't afford to miss something."

"Okay, let's talk about Becky Paul. Music teacher. Married with two children. Goes to class some...what...thirty miles away in the dark twice a week?"

"More like thirty-five. But lots of folks take college classes at night. And that's about the only way to get from where she works to the college, unless she goes way out of her way. She's been taking classes for at least two years and never had an incident, according to Steve."

"Everybody seems to like her and no one feels like she has enemies either. But both Becky and John are dead. Violently."

"If you want to talk about violence, get to the black woman. My God, that's unbelievable. I've never seen anything like that." I had to agree with Chase.

"Joyce Beech. Math teacher. Mutilated. Why so much violence? Why are all these people involved in education in some way? Why, if this is a serial killer, is he targeting males and females and white and black victims? Does he have a personal vendetta against these people or is he simply targeting school personnel? Are the killings going to be increasingly violent?"

"I don't see how they could get more violent than Beech's. Too many questions and not enough answers," yawned Chase.

"I do think the killer's geographically stable."

"Yep."

"All the killings are within a fifty-mile radius. I think we have a killer among us, Chase. He's walking around with us everyday. We have to be more observant. He'll get sloppy over time, but how many people will die before then? We're dealing with an intelligent, maniacal killer. We have to figure out the connection between these people. From now on everybody we see is suspect."

Chase suggested we send all school system employees an alert to use extreme caution and to go everywhere in pairs, and even car pool for added protection. I let out a mammoth yawn. We were both exhausted and had to rest before we could think straight. We stopped talking, got still, and fell asleep in our chairs.

23

Joyce Beech's father flew in for the memorial service. He'd fly the remains home to Chicago for burial once they were released. His head was as shiny and long as an eggplant, his eyes swollen slits of sadness.

"She thought coming to North Carolina to teach would bring her a better life," he said, wiping the sweat off his bald head. "And she loved it, too, I mean every week she called, full of excitement about what her kids did in school." He bowed his head, shaking it.

"Mr. Beech, how long has she been teaching here?"

"I guess it's been three or four years now."

"Did she ever mention having problems with anyone? She was a black female in a predominantly white area. Did she ever mention any racism or harassment?"

"No, and that surprised me. I expected her to come running home with her tail tucked, but she never did. She was a loner, Agent Hunter. She never mentioned close friends or enemies. Do you think this could have been some madman just passing by and grabbing her 'cause she was home alone, way out there by herself?"

"No, sir. I'm sorry. What happened to your daughter seems far too violent for a happenstance. I think she knew her killer and he was enraged about something. Maybe a love affair?"

"I doubt that, Miss. I realize I'm up north and not into her bizness, but she'd have mentioned a man in her life. Always hoping to meet a nice man. She'd a told me."

I gave my condolences and headed home to take a de-stressing run in the pasture behind Taryn's.

24

I'd promised Pepper I'd come for the grand opening of her restaurant and the time had come. I packed an overnight bag, feeling guilty about leaving the investigation in turmoil. But a promise was a promise and Pepper would do it for me if the gun were in the other holster. She and I had been through so much together. I couldn't let her down.

I wanted to be in the restaurant before the ribbon cutting at nine and I had ample time, barring any major traffic congestion. I drove, studying the clouds as I often did when driving alone. Just before sunset the cornflower sky looked infested with murky alligator clouds, all with open mouths. I hoped it wasn't a bad omen.

I arrived at the new restaurant, Pepper's, she'd named after herself. As owner and executive chef, she'd settled in, but set the grand opening night on her thirty and something birthday. She showed me around and I was delighted she'd rebounded after the murder of her lover, my first criminal investigation. Through the ordeal we became the best of friends and kept in touch even though our careers were taking us in different directions.

I'd known about her plans to gut the colossal warehouse and turn it into the restaurant of her dreams, and she had the money to do it. I hadn't seen a restaurant like this anywhere in North Carolina. Her taste was elegant but not to excess. The massive building divided into rooms with rice paper partitions, creating an intimate ambience and allowing her to create a different sense of time or theme in each. The front lobby walls were dramatic forest green with shimmers of gold and wonderfully warm and welcoming wood highlights. The floor was the same warm wood.

I could see the Oriental room with vibrant red walls and shellac black tables, square dishes in red, black, and Carolina blue. Each centerpiece was a Bonsai tree, small enough to converse over. Chopsticks were standing ready in a tureen. Subtle Far East music filled the space.

The next room was Tuscan with roosters in warm golds and oranges with topiaries. The wood floor peeked around the edges of an enormous rooster rug. Big block wood tables were uncovered except for gorgeous scalloped plates edged in gold. The centerpieces were tiny live topiaries dressed with bows. A hint of Italian music swept by my ears, and I imagined I could taste Marinara sauce.

We moved into the Mexican room with its bright oranges and yellows, highlighted with dried hot peppers and authentic sombreros. A rug in bright stripes covered most of the floor, and runners of woven fabric that seemed to be dyed burlap topped each table. The center of each table had an arrangement of peppers in red, green, yellow, and orange. The music was louder than the other, and most definitely, Mexican.

The adjacent room was French, with brilliant blues and yellows in white floral prints, and white French provincial tables set with the most vibrant blue color I'd ever seen. The china pristine white and goblets sparkling crystal. Delicate music played softly in the background. I literally drooled over the atmosphere. Pepper giggled at my reaction.

"Wow! It's the most awesome place I've ever seen!"

She tugged on my arm. "Wait 'til you see the kitchen," she said, pulling me through some stainless-steel swing doors behind the next partition. The place hummed with activity, many cooks working on their assignments for the big event.

"Wowzeewow!" The entire kitchen was stainless, with rows of industrial appliances, huge glass-front refrigerators and freezers, gas stoves, and ovens larger than I'd ever seen, and even a brick pizza oven with a real fire.

"Everything has to be authentic. That's what we stand for," she beamed with pride. I didn't ask her how many people she hired to handle it, but I'd already heard the Triangle buzzed with excitement and people drove from all over the state for this dining experience. I was happy for her.

A cook handed her two plates with awesome triple-decker sandwiches, served with sweet onion petals she'd just battered and fried. Pepper and I nibbled in the 1950s area, near the front half of a 1957 Chevrolet, while the Everly Brothers serenaded us.

"I figured we'd better eat now. Then you need to dress. I've got lots to do before the doors open." I ate and enjoyed the excitement that filled the building. The sandwich was fabulous.

I changed into my new navy frock, adorned with only a few navy beads on the bodice, while Pepper double-checked the menus and assignments for everyone from the chefs to the doormen and hostesses with great animation. I followed behind her as she checked the gorgeous flower arrangements in each section of the restaurant, tugging on a few until they suited her. I felt like a puppy shadowing its mother until she turned and pinned a corsage on me.

"What's this for? It's *your* birthday."

"I'd like for you to greet people. You know, just smile and welcome them. The staff will take it from there." I must have looked dumbfounded. "You didn't think you were going to just relax, did you?" I met her grin with one of my own. I'd rather be busy than a wallflower at the dance.

She hugged me and disappeared into the kitchen. I stepped to the door to begin. The time passed quickly as the place filled to capacity with animated customers. I could hear themed tunes coming from each room, often inaudible over the lively banter and laughter. People were enjoying themselves and the place overflowed, creating a need for waiting-list numbers and vibrators.

"Good evening. Welcome to Pepper's." I'd made the statement so many times over the past hour and a half that it was automatic. I welcomed a large group as an upset waitress approached.

"Where's Chef? We've got trouble."

I moved her away from the crowd as a waiter took my position. "What's wrong?"

"A lady at table thirty-seven. I think she's having an allergic reaction."

"Take me to her." We moved quickly and discreetly to the table where several women leaned forward, checking on a supper mate.

I touched the lady's shoulder. "Are you all right, ma'am?"

She glanced up at me with her swollen face, broken out in a large bubbly rash. Her lips ballooned. She began digging at the rash on her arms. She shook her head.

"Call 9-1-1," I instructed the waitress in a soft voice. I lifted the lady out of her chair and moved her toward the main restroom where I'd seen a couch.

"I can't breathe! I...can't. . ." She crumbled in my arms and I eased her to the floor. Now everyone in the section was aware something was wrong. I knew Pepper would know momentarily. I knelt beside her just as she became totally limp. I checked for a pulse. There wasn't one.

"Somebody get these people away from here. She needs air!" Waiters moved people back. I began CPR as Pepper landed on the floor beside me.

"Logan, what..?"

"Allergic reaction to something." I puffed. "It's not your fault, Pepper." Puff. Puff. "I'll handle this." I puffed again. "Go back to the kitchen." I puffed and the woman coughed.

"Anybody got an epi-pen?" I yelled.

"I can't leave you with this," Pepper said, near hysteria. To my great relief, the EMS arrived with a gurney in record time. I stood, taking Pepper back toward the kitchen. "They'll take it from here. Listen, you have to keep things going. I'll go with her to the hospital. Her friends said she wasn't aware peanuts were in her entrée. She's highly allergic, but she'll be fine. She's breathing on her own now. I'll be back for the ribbon cutting. It's not your fault." I hugged Pepper and followed the ambulance, glad the hospital was a few blocks away.

Nine o'clock approached and patrons and staff gathered around Pepper, holding an enormous pair of scissors to cut the ribbon. The mayor and several other dignitaries stood beside her, and, once the ribbon was cut, the mayor gave her a key to the city and a dozen yellow roses. This was Pepper's night. Her dream had come true. I caught her eye from the back and gave her the okay sign with my fingers. Her shoulders relaxed as she beamed.

25

Chase and I started the day searching for evidence down the mountain from where Joyce Beech's body parts had been found, on the chance the killer threw the murder weapon or evidence over the mountain at the end of her property. We drove the Jeep with the top down, a pleasant morning, to search every roadside picnic area.

After several stops, we pulled into a picnic area, and while Chase checked out the grill, I wandered over to the mountain's edge, gazing at the glorious scene below. The French Broad River forked, divided by lush green velvet dusted with a blue haze. A hiking trail began just over the ledge. I lowered myself, about to step across two roots waiting to trip me, when one of them moved.

"Snake!" I yelled and scampered back up the incline just as Chase threw out a hand to pull me up.

"I don't think they're poisonous."

"They?" I glared as the other root wriggled off into the brush. Chase tossed his head back, laughing.

That's it! I'm getting new glasses.

"Logan, I think I've found something." Together we walked to the grill. Chase took a stick and stirred around in the old ashes. A partially burned shoe sole!

Why would someone burn shoes unless he'd done something wrong?

I ran to the Jeep and grabbed my evidence kit. He lifted the sole into a plastic bag and I labeled and sealed it. It would go to the lab just in case there was anything left on it to trace.

We decided to separate and scan the whole area for more possible evidence. I went toward the hiking trail with renewed focus as Chase headed toward a field of mountain oat grass, its green wisps long enough to easily hide a body or a weapon.

I'd gone some distance down the mountainside, using a stick to push down the oat grass ahead of me, when I heard him.

"Logan!" he yelled, "Help me!"

I scrambled toward the top of the mountain, falling once on the uneven rocks and skinning a knee. I rushed across the high weeds and saw Chase hobbling toward the Jeep.

"What happened?"

"Snake bite," he said, crawling into the passenger side with his knees on the floor and his elbows on the seat. Bloody discharge seeped through the back of his shorts and sweat poured down his face. I jumped in and spun his new Jeep around.

"What kind?"

"Rattler," he said, panting for breath. His chest heaved as if his heart would burst through the skin.

"Chase, you have to calm down. The poison will spread faster if you don't get your heart rate down."

Fat chance he can calm down.

He was pale and seemed disoriented. I found the main road and headed toward Asheville.

"No, t...turn around. Go to Hot Springs. Much closer," he whispered. I whipped into a gravel road and spun around.

"Where did it bite you?"

"On the butt, and no laughing," he responded. I wasn't. "Remind me not to eat greasy eggs," he almost yelled, throwing a roll of Charmin into the back seat. "I went in that outhouse and thought I looked. Logan, he struck so deep." His face was white, his voice weak. I watched helplessly as he collapsed on the Jeep's floor.

"Hang on!" I yelled, mashing the gas. The miles seemed endless before I finally turned into the Urgent Care lot.

I snatched the office door open. "I need help here! Snake bite!"

Two men who'd been playing cards came running as I held the door. They extracted Chase from the floor of the Jeep. He attempted to help but was too weak. I followed them into the back room as they worked to intercept the venom.

"Thank God we keep antivenin on hand," the dark-haired man said.

"Yeah, I'll start an IV," the other man said. I stayed out of the way, but kept my eyes on Chase, now unresponsive.

"Get plenty of vials, James. He's full of venom and bacteria." James nodded back at the man cleaning the area around the bite. "Hang in there, buddy. You're going to make it." It hadn't dawned on me that he wouldn't until the man said that. But this was a dangerous situation, with Chase in shock.

As if reading my mind, James said, "You saved his life," scurrying by with both hands filled with more vials. I paced the floor. Seconds dragged into what seemed weeks until they told me he would make it. My eyes filled with tears as I nodded.

"Are you family?"

"No," I muttered. "We're investigators working on a case together."

"You may want to call his family. We've called in a unit to take him to the Poison Control Center in Asheville. They'll probably keep him for observation. Venom is excreted in the urine. We'll keep him on IV and catheter until the poison clears his body. It shouldn't take long since we've given him a potent solution."

"Thank you so much," I said, compelled to hug the dark-haired man. "What's your name?"

"Hank. And that's James over there," he said motioning to his colleague. "I'm glad we could save him, but he may have some local tissue damage that will need attention."

"What do you mean?"

"A canebrake rattler bite is bad enough, but being struck in the buttocks makes it even worse. It's one of the few areas that can't be compressed even if you had a first aid kit with you. That leaves the poison to collect in the tissue near the bite. He may have to have some skin grafts."

The unit arrived just as Chase roused. His humor, though scanty, returned.

"I now have a new understanding of the phrase 'Bite my ass'." We hugged and laughed with great relief. I kissed him, full on the mouth, tears streaming down my cheeks. It just seemed the natural thing to do.

"Thanks" was his faint response as he touched my wet cheek, the medication taking effect.

Chase conked out and I called Sheriff Yandle to fill him in on the shoe sole and Chase's predicament. "Do I need to call anyone for him? Parents? Girlfriends?"

"I'll call his folks, Logan. And, no, there's no girlfriend as far as I know."

~~~~~

I let Taryn know I'd be at the hospital with Chase until he was totally out of the woods but when the nurse came in to tell me his parents were on the way, I reluctantly eased out, feeling a little out of place. I wanted to say so much to him, to keep him in sight, but I was, after all, just a colleague. Nothing more. A partner in a criminal investigation, albeit a concerned one.

The hospital released Chase after three days, but he refused to go home with his mother. I didn't think he should be alone way up the mountain at his cabin until he gained strength, so with a little nudge, Taryn insisted I bring him to her house to recuperate. This pleased me. The relief I felt brought other emotions. I'd been terrified he'd die. I didn't want to lose him. I'd never felt this way about any man.

I settled a wobbly Chase into bed and went to the porch where Taryn was busy writing. She wiped menopause vapor from her glasses and unbuttoned her shirt.

"Hot again?"

"I stay hot all the time, Logan, but these flashes are like Satan turning up the furnace." I didn't know how to respond to that. I launched into more details about Chase.

"I was so scared. I've never dated much and haven't worked close to anyone like Chase. Taryn, I kissed him on the mouth."

She glanced up and grinned. "It's about damn time. What took you so long?"

I'm sure I appeared sheepish as my confession gave way to embarrassment. "He's a fine fella, Logan. I've never heard anything but good about him. You'd make a nice couple. Just relax and enjoy it." She shifted. "But will you do something for me, please?"

"Sure."

Tweezers were in my face. "Please pluck these hideous hairs on my chin. I can feel them but I can't see them." She thrust her chin at me. I'd never noticed them, but they were there. There were three prickly hairs in close proximity. I snatched them out, trying not to hurt her.

"Thanks. I don't understand this menopause crap. I'm blonde. I've always been blonde. Platinum. These hairs are stiff and black. What the hell is that? Now I understand what 'not by the hair of my chinny chin chin' means." I giggled and handed her the chosen weapon. She, however, giggled not. "Look at my forearms, Logan. The hair is black and long enough for a curling iron. It's like my body has turned against me."

I felt sympathy, hoping menopause would be kinder to me. "Taryn, you're an attractive lady. You're seeing it much worse than it is. Other people don't even notice. Don't let this get you down. I'm sure it's only temporary." She squeezed my hand as though she needed to hear a compliment. "What are you working on?" She straightened the papers in her lap.

"I've decided to fill out this living will I've had for years. It's about time I did it. You can be my witness," she said pushing her reading glasses higher on her nose. "We've just had so much death lately. I want people to know my wishes, you know, in case something happens to me."

"Taryn, I think if anyone can live forever, it'll be you."

"I'll go ahead and tell you I'm an organ donor, every tissue, every organ, anything good enough to share. I think more people should consider being donors. A donated organ can make a little deaf boy hear the clink of a ball on the bat for the first time, or a blind child finally see a snowflake and a sunset, or a grandmother live long enough to enjoy her grandchildren. And, I suppose, a bald man could have some hair from my arms." She grinned. "I, one human being, can help them all. And, of course," she exclaimed with great enthusiasm, "I'd live on a whole lot longer that way."

I studied this woman in silence. What a beautiful picture she'd painted! I gave her a hug before easing by to check Chase, sleeping on his side, and heading for my room with tears in my eyes.

26

I grabbed my phone and poured coffee with the other hand. It was the sheriff. "You and Railey get over here. We brought in DeWayne Lamplighter for questioning. Some people at the post office saw bloody tools in the back of his Avalanche. He's prime." He said the lab report on the shoe sole indicated it was a regular work-boot sole, the kind blue-collar workers wear, and many students too. "Lamplighter's wearing some right now." I told him we'd be right there.

I rustled a still-groggy Chase out of the covers, telling him the news. His eyes immediately focused and he hopped up, remembering his sore buttocks a second too late. "Yeeow! That hurt!"

I latched on to his arm as he hobbled over to his trousers. "Chase, if you're not up to it, I'll go alone."

"No way you're leaving without me."

"I'll get you some coffee for the road. Meet me out front. Bring along a soft pillow."

The Avalanche had been impounded and Lamplighter yelled obscenities loud enough to be heard outside.

Yandle greeted us. "He swears he ain't killed nobody, but I'm holdin' him until we hear from the lab. There was blood and hair on his claw hammer. He claims he cornered a fox eatin' his chickens."

Big Thug yelled again. He jumped at the bars when he saw Chase. "You! I m..mightta known. You s..set me up, you b..bastard!"

"Give it a rest, DeWayne," the sheriff called out from behind us. Chase and I said nothing. We decided to let him cool his jets before asking questions.

I got my evidence kit and two pairs of gloves. We went over the impounded Avalanche, Chase removing seats and everything else he could when I asked him to. I collected prints, hair, fibers, and soil, just in case one of the victims had been in the truck.

Is DeWayne Lamplighter a killer?

He didn't appear to be intelligent enough to plan and execute three savage murders and cover his tracks. My intuition told me he wasn't the madman we were after.

I couldn't find any links to John Roman or Becky Paul during the week he was incarcerated. By Friday the thirteenth we got the lab report. The blood and hair on the hammer was not human; it was probably fox. Yandle released Lamplighter, who calmly vowed to get even.

Roy Nesbitt escorted DeWayne to his truck and talked to him for at least forty-five minutes. I had to wonder what that conversation was about. Maybe the deputy told him to drop it and get on with his life, but somehow I doubted it.

~~~~~

Taryn left a note telling me she and Cecilia were meeting at the church after school to practice wedding music. Ceil's niece was getting married soon and she had been asked to sing several songs. Taryn often went to practice to listen and make suggestions. She directed a few weddings herself, but not as many as Ceil.

After practice they were going to Ceil's to pick out new wallpaper for the kitchen, recently damaged by fire. I was glad they had something to occupy them other than the murders. I figured Taryn would spend the night with Ceil. I kicked off my shoes and got a glass of milk and a homemade cookie before my phone rang.

"We've got some excellent fingerprints from Joyce Beech's house," Chase announced. "Maybe we're finally making some progress."

"Whose prints?"

"We got lucky. They're DeWayne Lamplighter's. No doubt he's been in her house." I told Chase I'd meet him at the station and we'd interrogate Big Thug together. I loaded my Ruger and strapped on my ankle holster before inserting the extra gun. We'd be running the show this time, and the gloves were off.

Yandle and Cole Bristol, another deputy, brought Lamplighter in, cuffed and more subdued than on his previous visit. He gave Chase the bad eyes and sat down hard on the straight chair Yandle shoved him toward. We stood silently for a moment before Yandle motioned us all out, leaving our guest to stew.

"Chase, I'd like Logan to see what she can get from DeWayne. He hates your guts. There's no need to antagonize him any more. I arrested him on suspicion of murder. It takes a lot to scare him, but he's pretty scared now."

We agreed I'd question him. Bristol left and Yandle and Chase stayed in the hall. I stepped into the room, furnished only with a wood table and several wood chairs. I'd never formally met this man.

"Mr. Lamplighter, I'm Logan Hunter, SBI."

He stared at the wall.

"Did you know Joyce Beech?"

"No."

"Why were your prints found on door frames, cabinet doors and drawers all over her house?"

He swished his big head to the left and to the right.

"Silence isn't going to get you out of this mess. Murder's a serious charge. You can talk to me or to the sheriff. Or maybe you'd prefer Detective Railey."

"K..keep him away from me!"

"Would you like Yandle to take your statement?"

"Lady, I didn't k..kill nobody."

"I want to believe that, Mr. Lamplighter, but Joyce Beech was viciously murdered, cut to pieces, Mr. Lamplighter, and your prints were all over her house. How do you explain that, sir?"

"I d..didn't do it. I w..wouldn't do nothin' like that to a person."

"There have been two other murders, John Roman and Becky Paul."

"I d..don't know 'em. B..bet you don't have no prints from 'em neither."

"You're right, Mr. Lamplighter. Only from Joyce Beech's house. But we're assuming right now the same killer murdered them all. Maybe you just got careless the third time."

"N..no!"

He stood. I put up both palms to calm him.

"Let's both go through this one question at a time."

He sat and stared at the empty table in front of him. I pulled up a chair directly across from him.

"Did you know Joyce Beech?"

"No, I t..told you."

"What were you doing in her house? She lives in an isolated area."

He squirmed and groaned, trying to get out of the cuffs. I hoped they'd hold his huge hands.

"Mr. Lamplighter, you've been arrested on suspicion of murder. If you didn't kill her, why were you in her house?"

"You ain't gonna l..let me go, are you? You're g..gonna blame me for all them killin's, aren't you?"

"Unless you tell the truth. You're our best suspect."

Lamplighter twitched his face into a wad. "Pills."

"Excuse me?"

"M..medicine. I w..went to steal medicine," he confessed, turning red.

"What kind of medicine?"

"Anything. Over-the-counter stuff or p..perscriptions. Didn't matter."

"You got a meth lab, Mr. Lamplighter?"

His face was crimson. He hemmed and hawed a few seconds. "If I g..give you some information, will you l..let me go?"

"Not if you killed that woman."

"Are your ears w..waxed? I been t..tellin' you I didn't kill her, or n..nobody else neither!"

"How do I know you went to Joyce Beech's to steal medicine?"

"I can prove it. I go around s..stealin' stuff and take it...to a certain place and d..drop it off. I probably got a pill bottle with her n..name on it." He swished his cuffed arms around on the table.

"Where would it be? We've already searched your Avalanche."

"P..probably my trash. Behind my trailer house. I have an old r..rusty drum I burn trash in."

I went to the door and gave Chase the information, and brought back a soft drink for Lamplighter. "Do you steal from other people?"

"Yeah, just m..medicine, though. And before you say it, I've never b..been to those other people's houses."

"How do you get into the houses?"

"M..most people leave everything wide open. And I g..get the newspaper and read the hospital report. All them have medicine. I f..find out where they live. But I n..never hurt nobody. I go when they're n..not home."

Somehow I believed him. "When did you go to Ms. Beech's house?"

"A c..coupla weeks ago, I guess. Before I heard she'd d..died."

"What did you take?"

"Aspirin. You know, stuff for headaches and pain. She was t..takin' some arthritis stuff so I t..took it while she was gone to school."

"Your prints are all over the kitchen, bedroom and bathroom."

"Yeah. I c..checked the whole house. I t..tried to get all I could."

"Did you ever think of wearing gloves?"

"It ain't never b..been a problem." He dropped his head.

I continued to interrogate him until he came clean about the meth lab location. He wouldn't give up any names though. If he'd been in the house to steal, wearing no gloves, that would account for his prints. I still didn't think he was bright enough to pull off three premeditated murders, at least, not alone.

Chase returned with various painkiller bottles and a prescription bottle with Joyce Beech's name on the label. I gave him the meth lab information.

I thanked DeWayne Lamplighter for talking with me and told him I hoped we could soon release him, but he'd be charged with theft at the very least. I already knew we had no prints from the other two murders.

Madison County law enforcement swung into high gear with some extra deputies who'd been called back in. A plan was designed to surround the wooded cabin meth lab and catch as many people as we could. Chase led the charge and kicked in the front door. Three men and a woman were arrested. Roy Nesbitt reported that one man got away but he couldn't identify him. All evidence was confiscated.

Yandle released Lamplighter but told him he'd have a court date about the theft, and to stay in the area. He also told him to watch his back since he'd snitched on the meth operation. Lamplighter, pale and quiet as he climbed into his Avalanche, looked directly at me. "I didn't k..kill nobody."

•

In bed with your sistah? Get outta thar. Now! You don't never touch huh again. You's both my property. Mine!

27

One month later

He was pissed off with Cecilia Nesbitt, a Language Arts teacher at Forrest Middle School. He'd been watching her for weeks, waiting for an opportunity to get near her. She'd been spending so much time fixing up her house, and her art teacher friend, Kosterman, had been over so late at nights, he'd given up and gone home.

He watched Nesbitt now through his binoculars as she placed an ivory gown and negligee in a gift box before wrapping it with silver paper. She cut the tops of two large bows to make a fuller bow, then ran ribbon through each loop and curled it.

He was impatient. She'd be difficult to reach inside her secured home, but he felt sure she was going out. He wondered if the art teacher would drive up at any minute. They seemed inseparable. Hopefully, wherever Nesbitt was going this time, she'd go alone.

She'd just come in from having her hair cut at Fran's Styles and he'd laughed when he noticed it short enough in back to display the red stork bite on her neck. She seemed agitated about it. *That's what happens when you run your frigging mouth and don't pay attention, bitch.* He'd noticed Cecilia wasn't the most observant person and could be easily distracted. That would make her vulnerable. He grinned.

He'd run into her at the post office weeks earlier, and she got in his face in front of Ralph, the postmaster, and Margaret, a mail carrier. Nesbitt hired him to do some rewiring in the kitchen after her husband died several months before, and once he completed the job she paid him the full amount. When her kitchen caught on fire, the inspector said it was due to "faulty wiring" and she blamed him. She'd just wallpapered and painted the entire kitchen. She'd written him to demand her money back, and included a copy of the fire inspector's report, but he wasn't about to pay. He didn't do inferior work. The bitch wouldn't get a dime back. She'd left eight or nine messages on his answering machine but he never returned her calls.

At the post office he vehemently denied that his work caused the fire and he said he wasn't paying for any damages. He yelled at her and she yelled back. Ralph told them to take it outside. She said she'd get an attorney. But he'd make sure she didn't.

When she came out to her car, she had the present and an overnight bag. He felt the corners of his mouth curl.

~~~~~

People loved to talk around Trust so it hadn't been hard to find out Cecilia Nesbitt was taking a trip to Hot Springs. If he got lucky, he could catch the fat bitch alone, realizing he needed to be cautious since the SBI was investigating the murders. He wasn't concerned with local law, except maybe Chase Railey, but reinforcements required more finesse and creativity. He wasn't about to let Tall Skinny Bitch in a Hummer put him away.

He watched the shower festivities across the street from the outdoor gardens of Hot Springs. Some of the ladies were apparently staying overnight in the white stucco hotel. The bride took her time opening each gift, hugging the giver before moving on to the next. The well-dressed ladies drank punch, probably spiked, or champagne, and nibbled little table goodies, laughing, and enjoying themselves as only women can.

Cecilia Nesbitt dressed in a camel suit the same color as her dyed hair. Even her eyeglasses matched her hair. The only color about her was the red print scarf tied in a loose knot around her neck. She sang into a microphone, but Haze didn't know or care to know the name of the song. He did notice she made more trips to the champagne bowl than anyone else. He was pleased.

He decided to go and have some supper at the local greasy spoon and come back. It wouldn't be too difficult to find Nesbitt's red Cadillac in the small town if she stayed overnight.

Two hours passed before Haze returned. He was relieved the shower was over and most folks had left the pavilion and gone home or to their lodging. He wandered around the tiny town, deciding on a plan. He smoked a few cigarettes, being careful to put his butts where they wouldn't be noticed even by trained eyes.

He was glad he'd remembered to bring along the binoculars. He found her easily and could see her from a distance in her purple bathing suit even though it was dusk. With a gasp, she eased her rotund body into one of the famous private hot pools of Hot Springs. Once her body was accustomed to the heat, she slid on down into the pool. She'd waited until late to come, probably to avoid the crowds. That worked fine for him. Her tub was secluded and it was a cloudy night. Only a few lights flickered, and they were a considerable distance from her.

After taking off the sterling silver watch the future bride had given her that afternoon, she lay back and slid her shoulders under the hot bubbles. She closed her eyes. He waited until he thought she was relaxed. She didn't hear him as he crept across river stones in the shallow French Broad River. She didn't hear him slip up behind her and push her head under. He held it there until she stopped struggling.

~~~~~

Killing Cecilia Nesbitt had been too easy. She didn't even put up a struggle. He got no thrill, no rise out of it. She was probably too damn drunk to be in the tub to begin with.

He headed for his house, taking the high mountain curves at great speed, jerking the truck close to the mountain's edge in search of the missing euphoria. He was out of control and he knew it. Nobody could help him and he couldn't help himself. Killing was supposed to be exhilarating and he knew he'd kill again. Maybe this one, a dud, would be considered an accident. Nonetheless, he had ridded himself of another problem.

Once he got into his house, he put the sterling silver watch in his safe and hopped into the shower, pumping his penis until it was hard, enjoying the pleasure until the hot water and the hard-on were gone.

28

I heard the phone in Taryn's room right after I got into bed, and her response made me jump right back out.

"No! How? It's not possible. It can't be true! Oh my God!"

I threw the door open to Taryn's room and ran to her. Tears were pouring and she was becoming incoherent. I took the phone.

"This is Logan Hunter. What's happened?"

The voice grimly filled me in on Cecilia Nesbitt's accidental drowning. She'd been drunk and shouldn't have been allowed in a hot pool, but she'd apparently paid someone to let her go after hours to relax. Cecilia's son and niece had been notified and were on the scene. We couldn't do anything until the next day.

Taryn sat on the edge of the bed, her face buried in her hands, sobbing uncontrollably. She wanted to go now but I hid her keys and tried to console her, a futile task. I made coffee and coaxed her to the porch.

"Logan, Ceil was scared something like this would happen. You know, with all the teachers being killed. I thought we were all being paranoid, but maybe someone's going to kill us all!"

"No, Taryn. They said it was accidental. It's just a coincidence. She'd had a lot to drink. I suppose it could be negligence. I'll check into it. I'm so sorry. I know you loved her. Try to get some rest." I shoved two Tylenol PMs at her.

"Yeah, she did like a toddy once in a while. She'd told me she was staying over night to unwind and even invited me to go with her. Now I wish I had." Sobs continued as I threw a blanket around her. Taryn curled up in a fetal position and I stayed nearby.

"Logan, I loved Ceil."

"I know."

"Ceil and I were lovers."

"Yes, Taryn, I know, remember?"

She blinked and I decided to let her talk.

"She divorced some years ago and when my husband died, we spent lots of time together. I consoled her when her husband left her unexpectedly after cleaning out the joint bank accounts. He left her for one of the ugliest women in North Carolina. And she was a great comfort to me when Edgar died. We did so many things at the church together. I directed weddings and she played. We went out to supper or invited each other over to eat. We played some card games. You know, we just enjoyed each other's company. At some point—I don't really know when—we touched and that touch became a hug and a kiss. I don't know how to explain it."

"You've told me enough, Taryn. I never disapproved."

"I don't know what I'll do without her in my life."

~~~~~

The following day I questioned Roy Nesbitt, a basket case. Taryn told me he was a mama's boy.

"She'd been wanting me to stay with her at night. You know, because she was scared and I was scared for her. She already had this wedding shower planned for Ireland, my cousin. Mama sings. Anyway, she said she didn't want to drive after dark and it would do her good to stay over night and relax. I agreed, Agent Hunter. I agreed. I guess she drank too much. She does occasionally when she knows she doesn't have to drive anywhere." He teared up.

"Did she have any enemies?"

"Mama? Good Heavens, no. Everybody loved her. Anyways, this was an accident, right?"

Cecilia's niece, Ireland Tabor, postponed her wedding due to her aunt's death. I had questions for her.

"Why did she spend the night when she was less than forty-five minutes from home? Was she meeting someone?" Ireland said she wasn't aware that Ceil had a liaison planned. Her aunt seemed a little irritated but never indicated why.

"She drank a lot of punch. I asked her about it and she said she was spending the night and just felt like letting her hair down. She sang and she was supposed to do three vocals in the wedding. She has…had a beautiful voice. I don't know what we'll do now." She sat down hard on the stone bench and pushed her long auburn hair back behind her ears.

"Did she have any enemies?"

"Aunt Ceil? No, I'm sure she didn't. She was a sweet lady, Agent Hunter. Anyway, the coroner ruled it accidental drowning."

"I know, but with so many educators being murdered, I wanted to check it out as a possible homicide."

"I think you're on the wrong road this time. There wouldn't be any reason for anyone to hurt her. But there is one thing I should tell you."

"What's that?"

"I'd just given her a sterling silver watch. She put it on immediately. Of course, I'm sure she took it off to get into the hot pool, but it's missing."

I thanked her for the time and wished her well with her revised wedding plans. I had no reason to believe Cecelia Nesbitt was a murder victim, except for a visceral instinct, and this new information about a missing watch. There'd be another sad funeral to attend and plenty of consoling a heartbroken Taryn.

~~~~~

The little church couldn't hold the crowd, weary though people were of attending one funeral after another. Teachers arrived in vans and station wagons; many children came. Couples from all around the mountains who'd asked Cecelia to sing at their weddings sat stoically. After several eulogies and one moving story by Ireland Tabor, Roy Nesbitt rose and went to the microphone.

"Mama is still with us through her music." He pressed the CD player button. Cecilia Nesbitt's stunning voice came through the church speakers surrounding us with her version of "Amazing Grace." My skin tingled as Taryn sobbed and put my hand in a vise. It was, perhaps, the most poignant memorial I'd ever attended, Cecilia singing at her own funeral.

•

Quit cryin' over your maw. It's good damn riddance as far as I'm concerned.

29

"Taryn, my friend Pepper wants to come up for the weekend. At her grand opening she was too busy to spend much time with me. Do you mind if she stays here? I hate for her to get a hotel in Asheville. Are you up to having company?"

"I'd be glad for it. Maybe she can cheer this place up. I'll prepare the other bedroom for her. When's she coming?"

"Friday afternoon and she'll go back on Sunday night. She doesn't stay away from the restaurant for long. Are you sure you don't mind?"

Taryn turned. "Pepper? Wait a minute; you mean the one who owns *Pepper's* in Cary? I hear she's fabulous!"

"In the flesh. She and I met at Genesis Beach when I was interning. We had some difficult times and became friends, I guess to keep us both sane. She wants to go to some kind of festival up here this weekend. Do you know what it is?"

"The Testicle Festival? You're kidding me! The chef's coming to the Testicle Festival?" Taryn threw her head back and guffawed.

"W...what?"

"Logan, you'll be in for a treat. I assume you're going with her."

I stared at her with the realization I, indeed, intended to go wherever Pepper wanted to go. I wanted to spend as much time with her as I could. "Do I dare ask what takes place at this festival?"

"They eat balls, Logan. Plain and simple. Cowboy caviar. Mountain oysters. Highlands tender groin. Turkey nuts, bull balls, you name it, they cook 'em and eat 'em. They're considered a delicacy but I've never tried 'em."

I shook my head. Pepper had once mentioned having a recipe for fried bull gonads but I thought she was kidding. *She can't be planning to put them on her menu. Can she?*

Pepper followed my directions straight to Taryn's dirt path. I greeted her with a welcoming hug and grabbed a brocade duffel bag from the back of her Infiniti QX56. We walked arm-in-arm up the front walk into the house. "I love this place! Wow!" She responded to it the way I had.

Taryn came bounding down from her studio to meet the chef, wrapping her in a bear hug. Pepper gave me a startled glance. I smiled and shrugged, indicating Pepper should relax and enjoy the vivacious artist. I was glad Taryn was already filling the house with laughter again.

After a tour of the house, Taryn settled Pepper in a bedroom near mine so we could stay up all night and talk if we wished. We were grateful we'd have some private time together, Taryn having made plans to attend a movie in Asheville with a friend from her school. Pepper was relieved to have a couple of days off after hiring a sous chef she trusted to run the kitchen. The grand opening had been successful and she needed a break.

Chase came about six o'clock. I'd convinced him we needed an escort to the event and, since he felt strong enough, he agreed to get us to the festival even though he'd never been to it before. When Pepper saw Chase, she gave me a raised brow, obviously thinking, as I did, he was one gorgeous guy. Chase was sweet, and catered to both of us as we piled into the Hummer and let him drive. We sat in the back seat and chatted and giggled, occasionally bringing him into the conversation. The roads were switchbacks and we sometimes grabbed the bars for support.

"Chase drives these mountains like he's on flat land," I explained to Pepper, who was pale. He slowed his speed and soon came upon a parking area off to the left. We pulled in and locked up. Across the road, a white plastic banner twinkled with lights: *Go Nuts* at *the Testicle Festival.* I spotted a television cameraman filming cooks and getting reactions from tasters. People were bestowing glorious accolades on the samplers.

We approached the tables and a man shoved sturdy cardboard platters into our hands. I tried to give mine back, but Pepper pulled me toward a deep fryer filled with bubbling oil. Chase gave me a bemused look and egged Pepper on to get me to try a fried bull gonad. Unexpectedly one was on my plate, sizzling, and smelling—alluring. I shook my head. What was I thinking? I turned and watched in horror as Pepper and Chase counted to three and bit into a crispy gonad. They both leaned toward me, chewing and moaning as if it was wonderful, but they weren't fooling me.

"Eat up, Logan. They won't be this good once they cool off," Pepper warned. She and Chase both took another bite. Chase winked at me and walked off toward some boiled kudzu, adding it to his plate. I followed them with my gonad still in its entirety.

Chase handed me some sort of brew. "Here. Drink this with your meat."

I glared at him. "Chase! I can't believe you all are eating this stuff! How nasty can you get?

Pepper was beside us to explain that once the testicles are removed, they are skinned, and the meat is pink and clean. "Logan, you eat range chicken all the time. What do you think they eat? They walk around eating bugs and worms. This is much cleaner! Don't be such a prude. Have an adventure." She darted off toward some other concoctions.

I decided to appease them and after that go throw up over by the bushes. I screwed my face and sank my teeth into the fried bull testicle—still warm—and managed to chew and swallow, holding the brew Chase had given me close by.

Umm, tender. Juicy. It's not that bad.

It resembled a large Irish potato cut length-wise and fried with the peel on. It didn't taste like a potato but it didn't taste like meat either. A new taste, for sure. Chase pulled me over to some barbecued nads and we both plated one and joined Pepper at the turkey balls. They tasted like chicken nuggets.

I took a sip of the liquid in my hand and spewed it. "What the hell?"

Chase turned with a red face. "Um…straight rye whiskey."

"Are you seriously trying to kill me?"

Chase took the rye and replaced it with a soft drink I guzzled as Pepper stood by laughing. A cameraman approached us, so we ducked behind a tent and headed for the Hummer, ignoring his calls. Pepper didn't want to be seen on the news. It might not be good if her clientele thought she used gonads in her recipes.

Just as we stepped into the road, a truck came out of nowhere with no lights on, roaring straight for us. Chase grabbed me as I snatched Pepper back, but not fast enough to keep her from being brushed hard by the truck's fender, knocking her to the gravel. The truck never slowed as Pepper rolled on the ground.

"My God, Pepper! Are you hurt? Someone tried to kill us! Who was it, Chase?"

"Couldn't make it out. Too damned dark. No light on the license plate."

Onlookers surrounded us as we checked Pepper over.

"I'm okay, I think. Help me up and get me out of here before that TV crew finds out."

Chase and I lifted her and headed for the Hummer to take her to the ER for a thorough check. We were silent as Chase drove down the mountain with the hazard lights flashing as I comforted Pepper in the backseat.

"Do you really think somebody's after us, Logan?" Pepper asked.

I met Chase's eyes in the mirror. "No, Pepper. You know I sometimes have an overactive imagination. Probably some drunk."

"Yeah, too much liquor and nuts," Chase chimed in, winking at me.

Pepper had a contusion on her right leg and her elbow hit the gravel hard enough to skin some flesh, but she didn't have any broken bones. Relieved, we took her back to the house just as Taryn got home. We explained why Pepper limped, and she gathered a blanket and a down pillow to make her more comfortable.

We settled her into bed and Chase, Taryn, and I walked out to the sunroom. Was someone after us? Chase and I were the targets if it were true. Maybe we were getting too close and the killer was planning to eliminate us.

While Taryn made Pepper some hot chai tea, Chase and I walked into the field behind the house. He put his arm around me and was about to speak, but grabbed my arm and nearly snatched me back. "Hold still. Don't move a muscle."

"Another snake?"

He stared off into the distance. "Wolf. Got your pistol?" I snatched my arm away.

"No." I turned slowly to meet the eye of the wolf, in about the same place I'd seen him before. "No, we're not killing him. I've seen him before. This must be his territory."

"Logan, wolves are nothing to play with," Chase warned.

"I don't care. We can't kill him. He's beautiful. He's never caused a problem."

"It only takes once," Chase theorized, but we went back inside, curled up in the same chair and feel asleep.

I awoke to Chase's Jeep cranking. It was late. I felt my way through the big house to my bed after peeking in on my sleeping friend.

~~~~~

Taryn had a hot breakfast waiting. I collected Pepper and moved to the table.

"You don't have to hold on to me. I'm fine, Logan. I'm just a little sore." I released her. Taryn took beverage orders. It was good to see her energy and enthusiasm return.

"Hot tea, thanks," said Pepper, giving Taryn a warm smile. "She's so nice. You're lucky to have such a great place to stay, and Chase…well, if I were a little younger, I'd have to compete with you."

"It's nothing like that. We're just working these cases together."

"Yeah, right." Pepper smirked.

Taryn brought us blueberry pancakes with syrup and powdered sugar. She also set a pot of coffee on the table. "I have an arts festival in Asheville today so I'm fixing to load up and head out. Pepper, can you stay until tomorrow? I'd love to spend some quality time with you. It's been hit and miss. Oh," Taryn smashed her hand to her lips. "Oh, my goodness gracious, I didn't mean…"

Pepper and I giggled. "An arts festival? I still need plenty of art for the restaurant. Can we help you load up? Maybe I can pick out a few pieces? I'm not sure about staying over, though."

"Sure. I'd be honored to have my work displayed in your restaurant. You better pick before I go. Eat your breakfast and give me a head start on getting it together."

When we finished an ample breakfast we headed upstairs. Taryn handed each of us an armful to take to the truck. "It's nice to have help with all this stuff, I must say. I can't haul much down the stairs at one time."

I carried several loads downstairs while Pepper pulled out things she might want. then we loaded the rest into the Pathfinder. By the time everything was downstairs, Pepper had selected four large stained-glass pieces, several oil paintings, two quilts, eight grapevine wreaths, seven stitched prints, and two giant rusted tin weathervanes. She also went through the silver jewelry and got three sets she liked. Taryn was delighted Pepper liked her work and she didn't have to haul all of it to, and possibly from, the show. Even though Taryn argued, Pepper wrote her a check for two thousand dollars.

"Keep it coming, Taryn. I love this stuff," Pepper exclaimed, after Taryn gave her another bear hug and climbed into the truck.

"If I don't see you again, come back soon, Pepper."

We waved her away, and I helped Pepper load the pieces into her Infiniti. We both took showers before heading to Saluda and Hendersonville to shop. Then we were going to Chase's cabin for a supper he promised to prepare all by himself.

30

He hung around Cypress Lane, the street carpentry teacher, Hank Iroc lived on, hoping for an opportunity to pay his disrespect, sick and tired of Iroc stealing his business. More and more people were turning to him for carpentry work, especially new folks to the area who didn't know Haze's reputation. Hank's work didn't compare to what he could do. Hank used patterns and still made mistakes. Haze could listen to what a customer wanted and build it to the customer's astonished satisfaction without a pattern.

Haze knew Iroc sometimes worked at Dulcimer High School even though it was now summer. He watched Hank's wife Glenda and son Dean leave for College Day at Western Carolina University, where Dean wanted to go in the fall. They'd be late getting home, so Hank would probably lose himself in his woodworking. Haze watched Hank load a few things in his F150. He followed at a distance as Hank stopped for gas before heading to Dulcimer. Iroc drove up the school hill and around to the shops while Haze took his time, making certain no one else was around and that Iroc hadn't spotted him.

Haze knew the Open House was coming as soon as school started up again, and he also knew projects from the last school year were incomplete. Haze would never have allowed incomplete projects. The kids would have worked all night if they had to. Iroc was a wimp. He let the kids tell him when they'd finish. Haze knew working in the school shop was one of the carpentry teacher's favorite activities, second only to his shop at home. He often did projects for faculty members or for the church, projects Haze was called to do before Iroc moved there from New York.

He hurt Haze's paint business and small repairs, too, like replacing screened porches and installing storm doors. He'd even seen Iroc repairing gutters. *He's a damned Yankee, that's what he is.* Haze eased his truck around the edge of the building and stopped. Iroc parked just outside the shop and locked himself in, like a scaredy cat. Well, he *should* be scared.

Haze watched through the tiny glass door window as the teacher grabbed various woodworking tools and lost himself in his trade, his lips curling upward to crease around his puffed mole. Just as Haze equity turned the doorknob, Iroc stopped and began to search the room, grumbling aloud to himself something about not being able to find his good sander.

He eventually picked up an old electric sander even though it probably didn't meet safety standards, plugged it into the outlet, and started to get the rough edges off a student's bookcase.

Haze, relieved that Iroc had not noticed him, carefully unlocked the door and slipped in to survey the situation from a better vantage point than the door window allowed. The loud sander created so much sawdust that Iroc pulled goggles over his eyes. He never noticed as Haze found a metal bucket and filled it with water, taking it to the outlet where Iroc had plugged in the sander.

Haze wore thick electrical gloves as he positioned the bucket and jumped back when the long cord hit the water, sending jolt after jolt through Hank Iroc's unsuspecting body.

"Burn, baby, burn!" Haze yelled as he watched the fireworks with a grin. Iroc wouldn't be stealing any more of Haze's woodworking business. No siree.

Haze left, not bothering to unplug the sander or remove the water bucket. Doing that would arouse suspicion, now wouldn't it?

He guffawed once he got to his truck. Customers would be flocking back to him now that his competition was out of the way. He drove down the campus hill, massaging his crotch and enjoying the pleasure immensely.

•

Git that thar calf outta the fence afore I turn the 'lectricity back on and watch you jolt, you mangy good-for-nothin'.

31

Getting to Chase's cabin was an adventure in itself with switchback after switchback, going up a hill where the road seemed to end only to drop hundreds of feet per second. I drove slower than usual due to Pepper's tendency to get motion sickness. Once we left the highway and took the gravel path, I could hear the *eek eek* of limbs hitting the Hummer. I slowed for the narrow path, envisioning scratches to the copper finish, wishing I'd let Chase pick us up in his Jeep instead of driving myself. Several colorful roosters ran off the path in front of us.

Pepper grinned. "He said it was in the boonies."

I slowed more as she pointed to the cabin on stilts almost hidden by trees. I circled a tree into the gravel drive.

I really liked Chase's cabin. Rustic and masculine. No traffic, too far from civilization for that. No phones unless you had a cell with a tower near by. Just peace and quiet. Chase said his grandfather built it as a hunting cabin. And a place for solitude and reflection, no doubt. I could feel it. The two-story exterior, constructed of vertical lumber, contrasted nicely with the interior planks that ran horizontally.

Pepper loved Chase's cabin as much as I did, especially the huge hot tub just off the back deck near the grill. The kitchen was a microwave, a toaster oven, and a sink-stove-fridge combination that took little space.

"I live alone. No self-respecting lady would live here, I suppose, but it's fine for me." He had a table, a futon, a satellite dish, of course, and the loft was his master bedroom, tastefully decorated.

The sound of a fast-moving stream beckoned us around the side of the cabin and down a bouldrous cliff. Pepper and I wandered the mountains and valleys all afternoon and waded in the icy stream, laughing and giggling like two schoolgirls. It felt good. We'd been through some stressful times together so this was a genuine pleasure, brought to us by the wonderful Chase Railey, who was preparing a feast at the cabin, unconcerned he was cooking for a five-star chef. We wondered what he was whipping up on his combo for us. It smelled divine.

Back on the porch, we listened to chirps and tweets as unexpected breezes tickled bare toes. From the porch I could see rolling lush valley, coming to a stop where mountains jutted up.

"I hate to go back to all the traffic and noise. This is heaven," declared Pepper. As if on cue, several deer stepped out of the forest and meandered over to the apple trees, munching on any trace of fruit they could find on the ground.

The moon came over the precipice as we ate barbecued quail, venison stew, and baked beans, topped off by Chase's exceptional chocolate pie, serenaded by the harmonizing of frogs and crickets near the stream.

"A great cook and a great look," Pepper spouted after too many beers. Chase and I made eye contact and he blushed. "I want this recipe, Chase."

"I'll send it to you. It's called Chocoholic Pie. I figured you girls would go for it." We did.

32

Pepper left on her trip east after a night of stories and laughter back at Taryn's house. Taryn left us alone except for bringing us steaming mugs of hot cocoa, elated over the number of sales she'd had. It had been wonderful to spend time with Pepper. In the early morning light I went to the porch to see the wolf. I could sense him, but the fog made it impossible to be sure.

I drove cautiously to meet Chase at the Sheriff's Department and we settled in with a coffee pot and cookies to spend hours going back over the same scenarios and drawing no conclusions. It was frustrating. The day dragged like a dog scratching its ass in the grass. I stared at my watch trying to wish the passage of time; the second hand didn't appear to be moving. The clock on the wall tick-tocked at what seemed half tick.

Unexpectedly Chase jumped up and pulled me to my feet. "You got a bathing suit?"

"Yeah. Why?"

"We're going water sliding," he announced. "Hurry and get your suit and we can stop by my place and get mine on the way."

"Chase, we've got too much work to do. We aren't anywhere near solving these murders."

"Logan, we aren't thinking straight. We're staring into space, not making any progress. You and I are both frustrated. We need some relaxation and a little fun in this madness. Maybe we'll get paged while we're out."

I wasn't sure; I didn't like leaving the cases to do something personal. I guess I felt we owed the victims and their families all our time. But Chase was right. Besides, we had to wait on lab results.

I rode with him, dashed off to my bedroom at Taryn's and threw clothes everywhere trying to find my suit. I hadn't needed it since my arrival several months earlier.

I made myself comfortable on the cabin porch while Chase hunted down his bathing suit. The peacefulness calmed me and I breathed a long sigh, mesmerized by the stream. A rustling noise turned my eyes to a doe and fawn stepping out of the woods, flicking their tails. They stood still and watched me watching them. I remained motionless. Soon they moved to the apple tree and nibbled until Chase's loud footsteps scared them back into the green lush.

When we arrived at Looking Glass Creek, he pulled over near the bathhouse and we changed our clothes. Many drenched folks came in to change back into their dry clothes. Chase and I darted up Sliding Rock, holding the metal rail installed just for that purpose. The water from the creek spread into a thin sheet as it spiraled down the sixty-foot slick rock to a deep pool below.

We held hands and sat in just enough water to get us started. We hit the pool at the same time and lost our grasp. The water was as cold as a warlock's dick, and I lost my breath. Once I found Chase, we climbed the rock again. After five slides, we bobbed around in the pool since most people were leaving.

"So what do you think of our version of a water slide?" Chase questioned, grinning like a schoolboy.

"I love it! Now I'm cold and starved, and you're buying." I pulled him out of the pool.

He laughed as we dried ourselves and went into separate houses to dress. We headed to Asheville to eat at the *Outback Steakhouse*. I called Taryn and told her not to cook for us.

The heavy meal made us both lethargic but we headed back up the mountain, knowing we couldn't continue to delay the investigation. Right outside the city limits, both sides of the road were filled with cars and trucks of every kind.

"I forgot about the Whimmy Diddle Contest," Chase exclaimed.

"The what?"

"The World Gee-Haw Whimmy Diddle Competition. We'll just stay a minute," Chase repeated as he pulled over into a narrow dirt path.

"Chase, we've got to get back."

"Don't get your panties in a wad. We'll only stay a minute."

We got out and crossed the road. I had no idea what I was about to see. Chase explained that a gee-haw whimmy diddle was an Appalachian folk toy, a stick of notches cut in one side and some weird propeller in the other. Another stick was inserted to rub the notches, causing the propeller to turn.

I couldn't figure out how this became a competition as Chase guided me to a small stage where a prize was awarded to the contestant who could make a whimmy diddle gee and haw the most times in twelve seconds. Gee meant the propeller turned to the right and Haw meant to the left. We watched for a few minutes, but seven contestants remained, so we stepped back from the crowd and walked toward the Jeep.

"Just a little taste of Appalachia." He beamed.

"Interesting, I think," I responded with a yawn. "Chase, didn't you say your parents live in Asheville? Do you ever go by to see them?"

He looked awkward. "Yeah, I sometimes meet my mother for dinner or supper, but not lately. I seldom go to the house. She goes to bed by 9:30."

"Why so early? Does she have to go to work early?"

"Mother's never worked a day in her life. No, she goes to bed at 9:30 'cause that's about the time my dad gets home from work."

I changed the subject. "Now's when I need the cold water to wake me up after such an extraordinary meal. I hope we can focus once we get back to Taryn's."

Chase bit a hangnail. "Logan, let's go back to the cabin and give Taryn a break. She's been opening her house to our investigation to the point I feel like an intruder. She's generous and I don't want to take advantage."

I shivered. The silence between us became deafening. Reluctantly I agreed, so we drove on to his place.

Once there, I grabbed a pen and notepad from his table and turned around—right into his arms.

"We need to talk," he said softly, taking the pen and paper and putting them back on the table.

Uh oh.

"Logan, I enjoy being with you, not just investigating but I enjoy you as a person. I hope you feel the same about me." He put his arms around me, holding me at the table. I tried to squirm loose. His hold got tighter. "Why the hell do you pull away every time I try to get close to you? Does my breath stink?"

Almost in a panic, I could feel the blood rushing to my face. "Chase, turn me loose!" He laughed. "Really. Unless you want to sing soprano, turn me loose!" My tone was nasty.

He released me and walked to the other side of the room, combing his hair with his fingers. I trembled. I didn't want this to happen this way. I did like Chase more than any man I'd ever met.

"It's not you," I said softly. "It's me."

"You're a lesbian?"

"No. No, I…it's hard to explain." I walked past him out to the porch and stared into the peaceful darkness. I could hear him walking behind me. And I could feel another presence.

"He's here," I whispered just loud enough for Chase to hear me.

"Who?"

"The wolf. He's here. In the fog, not too far away." I turned back to Chase and met his eyes.

"I can't kiss you because a wolf's out here? Logan, how can you know? It's dark as four feet up a bear's ass."

"A gut feeling. But you know, as strange as it sounds, he doesn't scare me. He gives me peace. I can't explain it. But it's the same wolf from before."

"I doubt that, although I've heard a wolf can travel up to fifty miles in one day. Why would he follow you? It sounds mystical. And you're trying to change the subject, young lady."

"Yeah, I guess you're right. But I like the idea of something mystical happening in my life." I sat and patted the cushion beside me.

Chase reluctantly joined me. "You're not gonna crack my nuts, are you?"

I shook my head. We sat and rocked the loveseat silently. "I understand why Raina likes this place so much."

"Where did that come from?"

"You said the two of you had a thing for each other."

"Had. Past tense. I got over it; she didn't. I talked to her about her goon of a boyfriend. Remember, I told you? She said she didn't mean for him to hurt me, but apparently she wants him to take a hike. Logan, I don't want to talk about Raina. I want to talk about us. I'm attracted to you and I thought, well, maybe you felt the same about me."

"I do, but life is complicated. I need to share something with you. Something I've never told anyone."

He squirmed and put his fingers to my lips. "You don't have to tell me anything. I acted like a brute. I'm sorry. We can take it slow."

"It's okay." And it was finally time to tell someone the secret I'd kept to myself for over seven years. "I've never been with a man. Except...I was raped in high school, Chase." Finally I'd said it. Chase blinked.

"I was a senior and he was out of college. My parents didn't want me to go out with him, but I assured them he was a nice guy. Boy, was I wrong." I gulped down some drink he offered me. "The date started off great. We went out to supper and met up with some of his friends. But later he drove to a wooded area and parked, and pulled at my blouse." Tears sprung into my eyes.

"Logan, stop. It's too painful. Just stop. I don't need to know this."

I couldn't stop. I had to say it all out loud for myself. I needed the relief I hoped it would bring. "I fought him, but he shoved me under the steering wheel and pinned me down. I know how to defend myself now, but I didn't then." I began to sob. Chase enveloped me and rocked back and forth with me until the painful memories subsided.

"I'm sorry. Rape should never happen to anyone. Where is he? He went to prison I hope. After he had to face the music."

"No, Chase. No music. I never told my parents."

"You let him get away with it? Logan, what were you thinking? He probably raped more girls."

I moved away from him. "I always felt like it was my fault, you know? Somehow I caused it. I've felt guilty for seven years, Chase. I never dated again. I didn't even go to the senior prom." I felt the tears burning as they slid down my cheeks.

He stood in front of me, moved his arms toward me, and quickly retracted them, not sure what he should do. I moved toward him and his arms settled around me. They were comforting. I didn't need to pull away. We stayed quietly in the embrace for a while.

"Logan, it wasn't your fault. And I'd never hurt you. I hope you know that."

I did. I felt seven years lighter. I told someone, someone I trusted with all my heart. It felt good. The awful memory was out and over. I turned and drew his face to mine. A kiss, long, soft, tender. It was enough for the moment.

"I'll fix us a real drink," Chase whispered. I was already relaxed. He did that to me.

I opened the screen, walked into the mist a few steps and stood still, sensing the wolf just beyond my vision. But he and I made eye contact through the mist. I could feel it. I smiled as a liquid peace moved through my long body. I eased back to the porch and Chase handed me a drink.

"I don't suppose he'd eat you. He'd rather have something with a little meat on it," he kidded, sticking his fingers to my ribs.

"Do you think I'm too skinny?"

"No, Logan, I think you're just right. I was giving a wolf's perspective."

"And you're not a wolf?"

"No, I'm not a wolf. I have great respect for women, especially you."

I knew that. I curled up beside him, sipping my drink and letting him gently swing the love seat. "What is this?"

"Long Island Ice Tea," Chase announced, touching his little finger to my nose. I kept my face lifted toward his. He planted another gentle kiss on my lips. I could feel the tingle in my groin I'd heard people talk about, that I, at twenty-five, had never felt. I pulled him closer and we kissed lightly, then more passionately until Chase pulled away.

"Logan, we need to stop. You're exciting me."

That, I had to be honest, was my intent. I set down our drinks and reached for him.

"Are you sure? I don't want to make a mistake we'll regret."

"I'm sure, Chase. I trust you." We caressed and explored with our fingers, the sensation electric even through my clothes. We moved slowly. Chase didn't want to scare me and I didn't want to regret having sex with this man, whom I cared more about with each passing day.

Gradually we moved to his futon and he took off his shirt, revealing the body I'd seen at Looking Glass Falls. Hard, muscular, hairless, sexy. My thighs tingled. I reached for my buttons and Chase pulled my hand away.

"Are you sure, Logan? We can stop right here. If we go on, I'm not sure I can stop," he warned.

I kissed his forehead, his cheek, and his lips, parting to let me in. I wanted him, and for the right reasons. I was falling in love with him, something I'd secretly vowed not to do.

Chase unbuttoned my shirt and bent to kiss the hollow of my neck. He moved to my shoulder and slipped the shirt off. I felt it ease down my arm and I wriggled out of the other sleeve, not losing focus on the sensations he created. I reached for his firm chest, rubbing my hands tenderly over it as we kissed, long, lovely kisses. I was abruptly aware of heat, passion's heat. We began to move faster, Chase unclasping my shorts as I unzipped his. We lay on the opened futon with nothing between us but passion that had to be answered.

33

When my cell rang at two in the morning, I knew something was wrong. I grabbed it and mashed *Talk*, expecting Chase at the other end. An unfamiliar voice responded instead.

"Ms. Hunter, this is the North Carolina Regional Medical Center in Wilmington." My heart stopped. "Are you the daughter of Nell Hunter of Wilmington?"

"Y...yes."

"She's been brought into the hospital and I'm notifying her family. Are you the only living relative?"

I could hear her even though the blood thumped through my ears. "Yes. No, she has two brothers and two sisters. What's wrong?"

"Your mother has been admitted with heart problems. Can you come?"

I thought of the killings for an instant. "Yes, but I'm on the other side of the state. It'll take six hours if I leave now. Is she in CCU?" I grabbed my brocade duffel when Taryn walked in.

"No, she isn't critical, but she's asking for you."

"Please tell her I'm on the way. Can you give me a phone number?"

The lady gave me a direct number to the hospital room but said my mother was on oxygen and IV so unless the phone was close, she might not answer. I thanked her.

"What's wrong, Logan?" asked an alarmed Taryn.

"My mother. In the hospital. Not critical, so I guess that's something, huh?" I trembled.

"What can I do? I'll go with you."

"No, I don't have any idea how long I'll be gone. But, Taryn, please call Chase. I hate to leave him with all this investigation, but…"

She helped me throw some things in my duffel. She threw me toothpaste, brush, and deodorant. I snatched two pairs of jeans and two shirts off the hangers.

"I'll call Kent Poletti on the way. It'll be daylight before I get to Wilmington. Maybe I can make better time during the night."

Taryn hustled me to the Hummer and gave me a hug. I wheeled around and spun out the drive, heading east, having no idea what to expect once I arrived at my destination.

~~~~~

Mama was sleeping when I got to her room at 7:12. I'd made great time until I hit the Wilmington morning traffic near the hospital exit. Finding a parking space big enough for the Hummer was another feat. I walked over to the unfamiliar woman in the bed. She looked terrible, her face as white as her thin hair, the flesh around her eyes eggplant purple. It shocked me how much she'd aged in four months. I sat quietly and watched my mama's heart grab her chest and snatch it up only to throw it down and start again. This went on for hours. I had to wonder how her heart could be so strong, beating on even though the rest of her body tried to abandon ship.

I'd been a menopause surprise, Mama having been told repeatedly she couldn't have children. I appreciated, now that I was older, all the tiny dresses she smocked or tatted, in spite of the arthritis pain. I'm sure she must have been disappointed when I turned into a tomboy around the age of ten, shooting B-B guns with the boys on the block and climbing trees with the best of them.

"Logan," came the weak voice.

I reached for her frail hand, deep purple from being pricked countless times to find a vein. "Hey, Sleepyhead," I whispered, kissing her forehead.

"I don't know what happened. They said I fell. I don't remember. Did I break?"

"No, Mama, you didn't break, but your heart's not in rhythm. They call it atrial fibrillation. They're doing tests to find out if you can tolerate surgery to install a pacemaker. You seem to have a good team of doctors. They're in and out of here all the time. I like your nurse too. He's strong enough to change your bedding without disturbing you."

"Yeah, I like him too. I've never had a male nurse. He's gentler than the women. I can't seem to do anything for myself, Logan. I'm useless."

"Mama, you're not useless. You're just worn out and this heart episode has taken a lot of energy. The doctor said he didn't know how you'd managed this long without some help. Your heart was beating so fast he said it fluttered, not actually a beat at all. You'll feel stronger as soon as they install a pacemaker."

I told her I'd met a detective capable of running the investigation without me. Even though I called her once a week, she wanted to know more about Chase and Taryn, the strange but delightful woman I lived with. I launched into a lively conversation about Taryn, her bout with menopause, and how kooky she was. When I finally stopped to take a breath, giggling myself, my mother was asleep.

The following day her medications were changed and she improved rapidly. She was to have the pacemaker installed once her blood levels stabilized, they thought, in about a month. They discharged her back to the retirement home and I drove her. Once she settled into her rocking chair by the window overlooking the lake, she started the conversation I always dreaded.

"Logan, you know I worry about this job of yours. I want you to find something else to do. I want you close to me, not all of over the country chasing down crazy people."

"Mama, you know I love my job. I knew what I was doing when I went into Criminal Justice. I'm sorry you don't approve, but somebody has to catch the crazies so they don't continue to kill and maim innocent people."

"But I need you here. I'll make some phone calls and see if the police department has a nice desk job. You can get an apartment around here and come to see me every day." I had to give it to her: she had always been able to push my buttons and make me feel guilty and lower than an alley rat.

"Mama, I'm not leaving the SBI. I just got in. And it's my passion," I said, trying to contain my impatience and deal with a woman who had always wanted to be in control.

"Passion, smassion—"

"Mama, I have the right to do what I want to do! I love you, but I'm tired of having this conversation every time I see you. Can't you just be proud of me and what I chose as a career?"

She didn't make eye contact or respond. After a few minutes, I stood up.

"Where are you going?"

"I have to get back to the mountains, Mama, now that you're doing better. I'll come for your pacemaker surgery in about a month. I'll call every week, as usual, and check on you."

"But what'll happen to me?"

"You have your 9-1-1 necklace. Wear it all the time. If you get in trouble, you just mash it, and someone will come right up and check on you. They have all my numbers so they can reach me any time. And I put three novels on the desk for you to read." Her face drew in like she'd sucked a lemon.

"You're just going to leave an old woman, your mother, and go back to the mountains?"

My jaw tightened. "You make it sound like I'm abandoning you. It's my job."

"I demand you stay here!"

"No, Mama," I said sadly. "I'll call you, okay?"

"No. No, it's not okay. Don't call me," she answered in a huff, her face still acidic. "I'll just sit here and wait to die."

I hated to leave her in this disposition, but I kissed her forehead and headed west with a heavy heart, not knowing how I'd find her the next time I came.

34

After a hearty meal and discussion about Mama and Cecilia, Chase and I worked at Taryn's kitchen table, piecing together the evidence we had so far. We spread out the information and reports of any trace evidence, going through every possible scenario, bouncing ideas off each other. We didn't mention our night together. I guess he could sense I needed some space to put things in proper perspective. I felt like my face was shining as much as my soul. I was fine. More than fine. Except for feeling guilty about my mother. I'd been on so many guilt trips I'd lost count, but I couldn't will myself to stop traveling. The baggage just seemed to get heavier with time.

Chase's pager vibrated and I turned off my unattractive thoughts as he flipped his phone to call in. I liked the speakerphone feature on it. I could hear every word.

The dispatcher spoke. "Detective Railey, a Mrs. Iroc called. She wants to talk to you about her husband's death."

"Who?"

"You know, Hank Iroc, the teacher who electrocuted himself at Dulcimer."

"Oh, yeah. Did she say what she wants?"

"No, sir, but she was some kind of upset." The dispatcher gave Chase a number and street address and he wrote it on the pad I pushed toward him.

"Wonder what this is about? The coroner ruled that accidental."

"Maybe she just wants to eliminate any doubt since so many teachers have been killed, including John Roman from the same high school. It won't hurt to talk with her."

"You're right. Let's go."

"Me?"

"Yep. We're a team. I'm not going without you."

I grinned.

~~~~~

The house at 1278 Cypress Lane was ranch-style brick with great curb appeal, neat, clean lines that welcomed any visitor. I could see a shop behind the house, painted the color of the house trim, also neat, surrounded by manicured lawn. We approached the front door as a woman came around the corner of the house wearing gardening gloves.

"Can I help you?" asked the attractive lady.

"Mrs. Iroc? I'm Detective Railey and this is SBI Agent Hunter."

She pulled off her gloves and shoved them into the work smock she wore. "Thank you for coming so promptly. Please come around to the back yard."

We followed her to a brick patio just off a large deck. "This is a lovely place. You must work in the yard all the time. It's so neat."

"Hank and I are both neat-niks. Please sit down," she said, motioning to lawn chairs and a bench. "Hank was also a safety fanatic. Everything in its place and a place for everything. I'll show you his shop in a minute."

"What can we help you with, Mrs. Iroc?" I'd learned Chase didn't like wasting time with idle chit chat.

"I'm sure you've heard my husband Hank was found dead in the carpentry shop at the high school. Dean, our son, and I had gone to Freshman Day at a college he's interested in attending next fall. We were gone all day. We got home and Hank wasn't here. He was supposed to work a while and grill some steaks for us later. He loved to grill."

She stood and walked away from us to wipe a tear. She turned to us and continued. "I couldn't reach him on his cell phone so I sent Dean to see if he had lost track of time." Her eyes filled with tears. "I...sent my son. I didn't go. My son found his father. Do you have any idea how I feel? Poor Dean hasn't gone back to school. We've both been torn to shreds by this."

"Mrs. Iroc, we're so sorry for your loss, but you know the coroner ruled it accidental. My understanding is your husband used an unsafe sander and the cord came in contact with enough water to electrocute him," I said as gently as I could.

"That's just it, Agent Hunter. Something's not right. Come on. Let me show you his shop." Chase and I gave each other a glance and walked with her to the shop. It was as she said, neat, organized to the hilt. "He kept his school shop just this neat. School wasn't in session. I can't think of any possible reason for a bucket of water anywhere in that shop. I've been over this in my head so many times. And the sander? He would never allow students to use a sander that wasn't safe. The only reason I can think that Hank would use an old one is he didn't want to get the newer ones out of inventory just to finish a few small projects."

"So, are you thinking somebody planted that bucket of water?"

She nodded.

"But who and why?"

"I have no idea. All I can tell you is with all the school personnel who've been targeted by some maniac, I can't rest until Hank's death is investigated more thoroughly. I realize you people are up to your eyebrows in cases, and I don't want to believe that someone killed him, but I'm begging you to check into this. Please."

Mrs. Iroc walked us to the street. We told her we'd do what we could, making a note to see if the Dulcimer High School carpentry shop was, in spite of the coroner's report, another crime scene. Chase and I called it a night but not before deciding to call Janah Zack about getting into the shop.

35

Morning came quickly and Chase arrived for the breakfast Taryn promised.

"You know you're spoiling him," I teased.

"Somebody's got to do it, right?" We giggled. Her contagious laughter echoed throughout the big house.

After breakfast Taryn headed for her studio and Chase and I studied the evidence again. My cell rang around noon and the tiny screen read: *Madison Cty Gov.* Sheriff Yandle was on the other end.

"Agent Hunter, I got a number for you. A psychiatrist called. She said it's urgent she talk to you. Her name is Dr. Aasia Sicklepod." He gave me the number, and before I could ask what was so urgent, I had a dial tone.

"What's up?" Chase asked, shoving a piece of Taryn's freshly baked sour cream coconut cake into his mouth.

"Some psychiatrist called. The sheriff says it's urgent."

"So they've found you," he quipped as Taryn came around the corner with her coffee mug and chuckled. I gave them a semi-evil eye as I walked to the porch and dialed the number.

"Sicklepod Psychiatric."

"Yes, Logan Hunter returning a call to Dr. Sicklepod. She said it was urgent."

"Yes ma'am! Hold please." An Eagles' tune played in my ear as I waited.

"Agent Hunter, I'm Aasia Sicklepod. I know you're working on the murder investigations in Madison County. I should've called you sooner, but my sources told me you'd questioned a suspect right after Becky Paul died, so I figured you didn't need my information."

"What? Who? What're you talking about?" I almost shouted, running back inside, motioning to Chase to get me a pen and paper. He scrambled across the kitchen to Taryn's desk and handed them to me.

"The murders continue. We need to meet, Agent Hunter. Can you be at *Abraham*'s on Merriment Avenue at eleven?" the doctor talked fast and seemed distraught.

"In Asheville? Sure, but…."

"See you then" and the call ended. I stood in a daze as Chase tried to pry what little I knew from me.

"It was such a disjointed conversation. Something about a suspect and Becky Paul. I have to go." Chase agreed. He'd accompany me but wait in the Hummer.

On the forty-five minute trip to Asheville, we recapped what we knew and what we speculated about the cases. My insides were in turmoil even though Chase drove the Hummer with great ease and pleasure. It wasn't his driving that bothered me; it was the anticipation of troubling news.

"We've got time to go by my folks' place. You wanna see it?"

"Sure."

He cut onto 240 and exited at Charlotte Street and took a right on Macon up a steep incline toward *The Grove Park Inn*. "Ta dah! The Railey residence," Chase said with a tone of…what? I couldn't determine the tone. Acerbic maybe?

"It's huge and gorgeous, Chase. Why take such a tone?"

"I don't mean to. I don't know, Logan, it's a long story. I get no peace here. My dad expected…no, demanded I go to law school. When I went into Criminal Justice he was pleased until I took the position with the Sheriff's Department instead of pursuing a law degree. He barely speaks to me, as if I'm beneath him. This is all a big fat façade."

"I guess he was disappointed. He'll get over it."

"He's had enough time to get over it, Logan. And it didn't help matters when I caught him with his mistress."

Ouch. He gave me a quick glance but I stayed quiet.

"We'll come back and visit my mother when we have time. She'd like to meet you. I've told her I'm working with the SBI." He gave me a smile that could turn an ice cream sandwich into hot chocolate.

The minutes passed and we arrived at the fancy restaurant and parked a block away. I left Chase with a short wave pocket radio and tucked the other into my purse in case I needed him in a hurry. I strapped my .25 caliber on my ankle. We were both a little unnerved and suspicious of everyone.

I entered the heavy wood doors as a slender figure in a dark gray suit stood up from a leather bench and approached. "Thanks for coming," the striking psychiatrist began. She motioned me to a small private area away from the main dining room. "I'm part owner but few people know it."

"Nice," I said, glancing around but refocusing on her. She closed the door.

"I took the liberty of ordering you some wine."

I thanked her, then plunged right in. "Dr. Sicklepod, what's this about?"

The woman sat down across from me. "Let me start at the beginning." I needed that. "I'm a psychiatrist and patient confidentiality is important to me, but if this information can help…"

"Go ahead."

"I treated a man some fifteen years ago who'd been horrendously abused by his father all his life, both physically and emotionally. It all came out when his father died and he apparently realized the depths of the abuse and created a scene after the burial, saying he'd dig him up and kick his ass. He was arrested for disorderly conduct at his father's gravesite, for God's sake. I had to do a psych evaluation. He was bellicose for quite a few appointments."

"Bellicose?"

"Combative. He was a smart ass, pompous. He expected to lie on the couch and rattle off some crap about his parents and get out of there. I finally got in his face one afternoon and told him he'd be coming until I cleared him or he was sent to a psychiatric ward.

"He could have hurt me and left, I suppose, but he didn't. He began to cooperate. I think deep inside he wanted to know what was wrong with him. Eventually I diagnosed anti-social personality disorder. Psychotic behavior."

"Did you cure him?"

She sighed. "No. He's a sociopath: self-important, obsessed, and if he doesn't get his way, he's dangerous. I can't cure that. I treated him for months and never had another incident. Then he just stopped showing up.

"Several years later his wife became my patient, a victim of his abuse. It's taken me a while to realize he might be the killer. It should've clicked when Becky died. I'm so sorry other people have died. You have to check this out!" She almost shrieked as I grabbed onto her shoulders, dumbfounded.

"Who? For Christ's sake? Who?"

"Haze. Haze DeBrew!"

Chase appeared at the door, having heard our yelling. "My hesitation has been having privileged information, but since Becky Paul is dead, I feel compelled to give you some information that may, or perhaps, may not, help catch the killer."

I sat up straighter.

"Becky Paul has been a patient of mine for years, since she married Haze DeBrew. She began seeing me when he roughed her up. She wanted a baby, he didn't. He wanted to control her every move and every thought. He was obsessed with her."

"He abused her?" I questioned.

"Emotionally, verbally, and finally physically. I convinced her to leave him but she was terrified. Her parents, rest their souls, eventually loaded her up and moved her out while he was away building a house somewhere."

"What happened to her parents?"

"A terrible wreck on I-40. I think they'd been to Missouri to visit family and her dad either fell asleep or had a heart attack within twenty miles of their home. A head-on collision. A terribly difficult time for Becky," she said shaking her head. "Anyway, I digress. Haze tried to reach her a few times to apologize and get her back home. After a while he backed off. She continued to see me because of guilt, fear, and grief. She was afraid he'd pop up and surprise her somewhere."

"But wasn't that years ago?"

"Yes. She married again and seemed genuinely happy for the first time since I'd known her. She lived for those two little angels of hers. I seldom saw her until about six months ago."

"What happened?"

The doctor sipped her wine but I didn't touch mine. "She came in hysterical one afternoon without an appointment. I pulled her into the back office and tried to calm her. She said she thought she was being stalked but couldn't prove it. She just sensed she was being followed. Haze told her he'd get her back one way or another. She considered it a threat. So did I. I told her to swear out a warrant against him and to tell Steve. She did neither."

I sat still for a second, taking it all in. I picked up the wine and guzzled it. "So you think Haze could have killed her."

"It's just a gut feeling. I know you questioned him right after her murder, but since the monster is still killing, I wanted you to at least be aware. I couldn't keep this to myself any longer. It might not be him, but what if it is?" I thanked her and hurried out with Chase. We ran to the Hummer and he drove with great speed and agility as I dialed Sheriff Yandle.

•

I said git them thar britches off. I mean it. Now! Quit whimpering like a pup. I cain't believe your mine no way. Your dick ain't no biggern' a dingleberry. You ain't hardly worth the trouble.

•

"The judge is outta town. We can't get a warrant until he gets back," said the sheriff, rubbing his hands over his head.

Chase and I both jumped up at the same time. "Whadaya mean we can't get one?" Chase hollered. "Sheriff, we gotta get in!"

"Now, Chase, you know we have to do this the right way. If we screw this up, this monster could get away with it. Just cool down some. We're all upset. If he don't know we know, he won't run or nothing."

"Yeah, but he could kill again while we're sitting on our asses."

I touched his arm. We both knew Yandle was right, regardless of how frustrating it was. I wanted to know. I wanted to move, damn it! Too much time had passed already. It was time to do something, because if we didn't corral DeBrew, there'd be another victim. Yet, the paper we needed for a legal search evaded us.

We decided to call Dr. Janah Zack. She met us at the carpentry shop. "I have to confess I had the custodial staff clean up in here after the coroner ruled Mr. Iroc's death accidental." Chase and I both grimaced and dropped shoulders. "I'm sorry. I had no idea this would turn into a criminal investigation."

"You couldn't have known, Dr. Zack. We're still not convinced. It's just that the widow is suspicious about a few things."

I ambled off toward the walls, looking for a faucet while Chase and the principal headed for the storage area that housed all tool inventories. I covered all four sides of the cement workshop. No faucet.

"Dr. Zack, aren't there supposed to be water faucets in the shops?"

"It depends on what kind of shop it is. There's a sink in the back of Hank's office for students to clean up before they go to another class, but he didn't really need running water in the shop for carpentry. Why?"

"Mrs. Iroc told us his sander cord came in contact with a bucket of water. I'm trying to figure out where the water was and why it was in here. She said he was extremely safety-conscious."

"Very much so. He even wrote students up for discipline if they didn't follow all the safety rules." She called to a man walking by the shop door. "Mr. Teasdale, come here for a minute, please."

An old gentleman stepped into the shop. "I was just checkin' to see if anybody was supposed to be in here, Doc."

"Mr. Teasdale, these are inspectors. Didn't you help clean up the shop after Mr. Iroc's accident?"

"Yes'm." He turned to us. "It was awful. You can still smell the burnt flesh. We tried our best to get rid of it. I might leave the doors open some, Doc, to let it air out before students come back."

"That's a good idea, Mr. Teasdale. Can you remember a bucket of water in here?"

"Yes. The cord was in that bucket. I can't figure it, though."

"What do you mean, sir?"

"First, Mr. Hank, he never had water around the tools. Because it was dangerous. The water is in his office away from the tools, where they cleaned up. But after Mr. Hank died, Dr. Zack got all us custodians in here to clean up. It stunk, and everything was covered with dust or, I don't know, ash, maybe. We wore masks, aprons, and thick gloves. That sander cord was still on the floor where the EMS had to turn off the electricity to disconnect it. There ain't no tellin' how long that poor man was hooked up to that thing." He shook his head sadly.

"Where would the bucket and water come from?"

"It seems to me somebody would have to bring it in from somewhere else, like another shop. The auto mechanics shop is next door and they have to have water for certain things."

"Where's the bucket?"

"We threw what was left away."

We thanked Dr. Zack and Mr. Teasdale and left, wondering if Mrs. Iroc might be on to something even though we had precious little to investigate at this point. I called Mrs. Iroc and asked if she knew of any enemies her husband might have.

"After you left, I realized you hadn't asked that question. I began thinking and I asked Dean too. I couldn't think of anyone at all. I mean, Hank was a good Christian man, good to everyone. But Dean said some fella came over here one afternoon when they were in the shop. I was shopping. This fella came into the shop, Dean said, and accused Hank of stealing his customers. I asked Dean what he meant. He said the man was also a carpenter and handyman and didn't like Hank infringing on his territory. Dean said he was ugly to Hank but it was only words. Hank told Dean to forget about it."

"Any idea who this man was?"

"I wrote down the name," she replied. I could hear paper rustling. "Haze DeBrew."

36

I stepped out of the Hummer and headed to the steps, still unnerved we couldn't search DeBrew's house yet. I'd spent most of the day at the ophthalmologist, now donning contacts instead of wire frames. I heard a motorcycle coming down the highway. That was nothing new. The mountains were full of them, but this one sounded as if it were slowing to turn in the dirt path. I whipped around as the yellow and chrome Harley with a sidecar pulled up beside me with a grinning Taryn riding it. My mouth flew open.

"What the hell?"

"I know. Crazy, isn't it? But an almighty fine way to cool off in this pissy humidity."

"You sure you didn't buy it for the hot flashes?"

"Logan, you're such a good agent." She grinned again. *Is that a bug in her teeth?*

"Climb on. I'm fixin' to take you for a spin. Get in the sidecar."

I retreated, waving my arms in protest. I remembered the only experience I'd had with a Harley and a huge bull, and I didn't want a repeat. "I'll pass, Taryn."

"No, Logan. Please," she pouted from under her blonde bangs.

"Do you promise to go slow? There are no sides on these roads and no protection on a bike."

She promised. I walked around to the sidecar and tried to wedge my long legs in so none of me was hanging out over the edge. I simply couldn't fit.

Taryn got off the seat and came around. "I was afraid those long legs would be a problem, so, you drive this baby."

She climbed in the sidecar so I ran around to get on before she toppled the whole thing. Taryn was no lightweight. At least this meant I was in control of the speed. We hit the road and took off up the mountain, taking the curves easily. A couple of times I bounced the sidecar off the pavement and Taryn grimaced, so I slowed the pace and turned around just a few miles up the road. I drove back past the Trust Grill so Taryn could wave while I turned red with embarrassment.

~~~~~

I decided to run off my stress in the valley path I'd worn, paying particular attention to the plush foliage I hadn't noticed on previous runs. I slowed my pace to observe tall bright greens bowing in the breeze. They were flush against the trees where the forest began, thousands of them.

How did I miss seeing these marijuana plants?

Surely Taryn hadn't planted them, but they were on her property. Another mystery to solve. I headed back to the house, taking long strides.

"Taryn?"

"Up here, Logan," came her voice from the studio.

I climbed the stairs two at the time. She turned from her sewing as I stopped next to her. "I found something interesting on my run."

She seemed puzzled.

"Doesn't your property go up to the forest?"

"Part of those woods are mine. Why?"

"You have marijuana growing. It's almost ready to harvest. It's apparently been growing for a while and I hadn't noticed."

She stood and walked to the window. "But how, Logan? Are you certain that's what it is? Surely you don't think I . . ."

"No, but how do you explain it? They either started as seeds from some indoor grower or seed seller, or from seedlings. How could someone plant thousands without your knowledge?"

Taryn backed away from me. "I don't think I like the tone you're taking with me, Logan Hunter."

"I apologize, but I've got to have some answers."

"I want answers too. I lease some adjacent land my husband once farmed but I have no interest in farming. I'll tell you what, I'll drive you around all my property lines and maybe we can figure this out."

I agreed but changed clothes first, strapping on the ankle pocket Taryn knew I had. I holstered my Ruger, to protect us if we surprised someone.

Taryn owned far more land than I imagined, hundreds of acres, some rocky and treacherous, some plush valleys and fields, some timberland. We rode to the next highway and turned into a dirt path that took us on a bumpy ride back to the edge of the forest. We got out and walked around while I pointed out illegal plants. Taryn drove deeper into the woods until they opened into a huge field of burly tobacco impaled upside down on sticks. These sticks were arranged in semicircles, creating teepees of the plants for air-drying before being moved to a burly barn for air curing.

"Why didn't whoever did this just fill up this field instead of going to the woods?"

"It would be too easy to spot those bright green plants from the air. The person who did this is smart enough to know they might go unnoticed near the woods. I expect the street value on all this must be astronomical. We'll have to determine how many acres of marijuana are ready to harvest."

"I promise you, I know nothing about this, Logan. My husband would roll over in his grave."

"Who leases your land?"

"God help me, Logan. I lease it to Cecilia Nesbitt's son, Roy. He asked me several years ago. He said he didn't make

enough as a deputy to pay his bills so he'd raise tobacco. I
did it for Ceil. Surely Roy doesn't know about this." Tears
began to trickle down her rosy cheeks. "I can't believe Roy
would do such a thing. He's a deputy. If he did, he's no
count."

"If he does know—which he must—he's a real nice
guy. He planted them on your property so you'd be blamed
if they were found. A dirty deputy."

"You mean I'm in trouble? I'm going to jail?"

"No, Taryn, but we need to report this right now. We
can say you found them and were alarmed. Let's go back to
the house."

I called and asked Chase to come over, without giving
him the details. I certainly didn't want the deputy in question
to hear our discussion over a radio and run, or retaliate.

We took Chase back with us and showed him all the
illegal foliage around Taryn's property. Chase figured that
of the seventy-five acres of fields, at least thirteen acres
were planted in marijuana.

"What would the street value be on that?"

"I'd say over ten million dollars. And that's more than
likely a low estimate."

Taryn's knees buckled while I blew surprise through my
lips.

"It's felony charges, all right. And I'm not that surprised.
Roy's different. He's a hothead and rather defensive about
any questions directed his way. I think he and Yandle have
had a few words, but Yandle isn't going to fire anybody. He
needs all the help he can get."

"He wouldn't even fire deputies growing drugs?"

"Oh, Roy'll be through if he did this. I have to tell
Yandle. We can't afford to hide this. Roy'll just have to deal
with it."

"This would have killed his mother. She doted on that
boy," Taryn noted.

~~~~~

When the extra officers arrived we crept slowly toward the shadowy field where our suspects were. We had lawmen in all the surrounding woods and at every path big enough for a truck to go through. We eased quietly over stumps and jumped small ditches with great stealth, weapons in hand.

"Freeze!" Sheriff Yandle hollered out. Roy and DeWayne Lamplighter were startled. DeWayne froze but Roy ran a few yards and came to an abrupt stop. He watched as the woods came alive with officers. He pointed at Lamplighter.

"I caught him, Boss! DeWayne's got the whole place covered with pot. I'll show you."

Yandle walked over to his deputy and slugged him hard in the face. "You sonovabitch. My own deputy! You're under arrest." Yandle grabbed Roy, threw him on the ground and put his boot about half way up his ass and left it there. Chase put the cuffs on.

I cuffed Lamplighter. "Nice friend, huh, DeWayne? He was going to let you take the whole rap by yourself." DeWayne seemed defeated. "You know the drill. Let's go. This'll be added to your other charges." I recited his rights and marched him to the cruiser.

37

Still waiting on the warrant to search DeBrew's house, Chase convinced me to go with him to visit his mother. She called to invite him over for supper and told him he could bring a guest. Chase said this was her way of finding out if he was seriously interested in a young lady.

"Are you?"

"You betcha!" He grinned and so did I, but the pit of my stomach was queasy. Meeting the mother. I'd already determined Chase was sort of a mama's boy, or at least, he *had* been at one time. I tried to relax as he pulled into the arched driveway and came around to help me out.

"Well," I teased, "I'm impressed so far." I pressed my blouse with the palm of my hand and took his hand as we walked up the front walk and rang the bell.

A butler opened the door and showed us in. "Master Chase, how good to see you."

"Hello, Clive. I'd like you to meet Logan Hunter from the SBI."

The British butler politely dipped enough to show respect and showed us into the library. A large mahogany table and leather chairs occupied the space. Several brass lamps were strategically placed around the room so one could read in any corner.

"Madam will be with you momentarily. Can I get you something to drink before dinner?"

We asked for white Zinfandel as high heels clicked in the foyer. A gorgeous lady with silver hair entered and hugged Chase, giving me a slight glance.

"Mother, I'd like you to meet Logan. Logan Hunter."

She extended her hand and I reached for it. "A pleasure, my dear. Fern Railey. Let's sit. One of you on either side of me." She patted. We sat. Mrs. Railey politely interrogated me for a while, asking about my breeding and background. Chase gave me the high brows occasionally. I tried not to laugh.

As we moved into the dining room, I gasped at the long table that could seat at least twenty people. Chase and I started to sit together but Mrs. Railey guided me to a seat directly across the table from her, another place set beside me for Chase. That left a setting at the head of the table. Chase shot his mother a sharp expression.

"Chase, don't get upset. Your father insisted on joining us. He actually figured a way to get home early tonight. Logan, you should feel honored. He's actually having supper at home this evening."

I caught the tone. Chase was antsy as a tall, distinguished man appeared in the doorway.

"Good evening!" His courtroom-voice boomed, a broad smile covering every inch of his distinguished face. He bent to kiss his wife's cheek and came over to take my hand.

"I'm Andrew Railey. Drew."

"Logan Hunter, sir."

"A pleasure, I'm sure." I didn't quite know how to take that tone.

The man turned toward his son. "Chase." The word froze in mid-air.

Chase nodded as his father sat down at the head of the table some distance away. Drew Railey launched into who he was, what he was, and how he got that way as food appeared at our places. I suppose pompous ass would about cover it—everything Chase wasn't. The other three of us sat and listened awkwardly until the butternut squash soup arrived and the talking ceased for a few wonderful minutes.

"Enough about me, Logan. May I call you Logan? Please tell us about you. I understand you're with the SBI. How intriguing," he said, glancing at Chase again.

I told them I was born and raised on the coast and joined the SBI after taking Criminal Justice and completing an internship that became a murder investigation.

"Did you get your man?"

"Eventually. It took a while." I didn't really want to get into all the specifics.

Chase's mother awkwardly cleared her throat. "Logan, isn't that line of work a little risky for a young lady? You could be seriously hurt." I wasn't going to tell her about the scar on my neck from an assailant or the gunshot wound on my arm from a glancing bullet. "It's a great career. I wouldn't be happy doing anything else."

"Another risk-taker. I see you're a good match for Chase. He's rectum linear too. He puts his buttocks on the line all the time, don't you, son? He'd rather pursue bad guys than put on a business suit," Drew Railey replied.

I glanced at Chase who seethed. "I go after the crud, drug dealers, killers, thieves, and when I finally catch them, you get them off. They're back on the street before the ink is dry," stated a sullen Chase.

Mr. Railey slammed his fist on the table, causing me to jump. "You can't expect Nesbitt to stay in jail. You know that. He has a right to an attorney and his day in court."

"He's a dirty deputy. There's no telling how long he's been dirty. We're putting our lives on the line every day with this…this dirt bag deputy, thinking he'll cover us, that he's on our side. All the time he's growing enough marijuana to service half the country, to the tune of over ten million dollars."

"He says the other guy, the Cherokee, is the ring leader and he got pulled into it."

"Bull shit! You don't seriously believe that crap, and you're still defending him. Yep, I arrest them and you release them. I wouldn't have your job."

"Don't get a pompous attitude with me, young man. What's so great about high-speed chases and hunting needles in haystacks?"

"It's called justice, Dad. Making a person pay for injustices to other people. You wouldn't know anything about that, though. You're too busy getting all of them off because it makes you such a great lawyer. You always find a loophole. Killers, thieves, and drug dealers love you. I don't know how you can live with yourself. I find my job satisfying because I get them off the streets and away from society."

"Whatever wets your panties," came the ugly retort.

Fern Railey stood, now as red-faced as Chase. "Stop it, Drew!" Turning to Chase, she said, "Your father isn't trying to pick a fight with you, son. Not tonight. Please. Let's be civil. Let's just finish our supper and move into the living room. Drew?"

She may have expected her husband to smooth things over. He didn't; he sulked. She stared at her plate, not eating. I wanted to crawl on hands and knees to the door and escape. No wonder Chase never came home.

The evening dragged on. Drew ate hardily and drank several flutes of wine seeming to revel in our misery. Chase and I sat waiting for a chance to leave without causing another ugly scene. Once the dessert was served, we moved to the living room, which was too ornate for my taste. I walked so close to Chase we couldn't be easily separated. We talked for a few minutes in cold, awkward sentences, out of courtesy to Mrs. Railey, I supposed, until Chase grabbed my wrist.

"We have to go," he said coldly. He kissed his mother as Drew Railey walked over to me.

"Come back anytime, Logan. It was a pleasure to meet you. Chase, you be careful out there." And he disappeared. Mrs. Railey walked us to the door and watched us leave, not offering any apology for what we'd just endured.

We sped down the highway, silent, relieved it was over. Awkwardness. Discomfort. I hurt for Chase. What a shame to have each parent discontent with the other. How sad to have a son as exceptional as Chase and not be proud of him. I reached for his hand, touching the top lightly. He responded, taking it into his. He managed a faint smile. I returned it. Chase was a survivor; he'd be fine. And, most likely, it'd be a long time before another supper invitation was extended or accepted.

•

Eat your breakfas' on the porch. You been pissin' in your britches again, hain't you boy?

38

I heard the motorcycle crank up sometime during the night. I raced to the back door, thinking a thief had found it. Taryn pulled up beside me.

"Outrageous night sweats. I have to have some air. I can't breathe. I'll be back." Before I could protest, she zipped down the path and onto the highway with no helmet. At least she wore clothes.

I sat on the porch listening for the roar to return. I picked up a magazine and read a long article on Julia Roberts and her twins. One hour. I paced through the house, from porch to front foyer, around the bedroom hall and back to the porch. Another hour passed.

Where the hell is she?

I turned left out of the drive, hoping she went that way. I passed Mule Creek, slowing to see if any tracks left the road. I headed down the mountain past Hope Cove Church and the cemetery. I'd gone about ten miles when I decided to reverse direction.

I sped back up the mountain, passing Taryn's dirt path, looking at both sides of the road. What possessed that woman to ride a motorcycle at night on these treacherous roads, and without a helmet? An animal the size of a chipmunk could toss her over the side of the mountain, and if she landed in kudzu, she'd die before we found her or the bike. I cursed.

I finally spotted her on a boulder near Grizzly Gorge. I jumped out to chew her ass but I could see blood on her face even in the dark.

"Taryn, what happened?"

"I hit a patch of gravel and it threw me. I'm fine, but I can't get the bike cranked."

"Good."

"Don't be like that, Logan. I paid a wad for that motorcycle."

I walked the bike over to a big bush and hid it until Taryn could figure out how to get it home.

~~~~~

We walked into the kitchen and I flipped on the overhead light.

"I'll get the peroxide and some cotton."

She sat at the table and I doctored her nose and cheek as best I could. Her nose continued to bleed profusely and I offered to drive her to the hospital.

"Heck no, Logan. I'll be fine. They can't fix a nose anyhow. I'll just sleep in my lazy girl chair tonight. I'm fine. Just a little sore. Get me a box of tissues and you go on to bed. I sure did enjoy the night air, though. The wind in my hair felt marvelous. I just have to train myself for what kind of surface I'm on. Loose gravel is not the same as highway pavement."

I made her promise not to ride the motorcycle any time soon.

39

The next afternoon Taryn was dressed extravagantly by the time I got home, in clothes only she could wear. Her turquoise cotton skirt had been hand-painted and fell to her ankles where tan sandals peeked out. She had a pale blue tee over which she'd put a denim blue jacket. On the jacket she pinned a gaudy rhinestone brooch. Since this wasn't enough, she also wore a wide brown leather belt, embellished with many turquoise stones to match bracelets on both wrists, and a multi-strand turquoise necklace on which she'd pinned a rhinestone cross pendant. She seemed excited and scurried around the room, loading some of her art into a red paisley duffel bag she'd made herself.

"What's up?" I asked, grinning back at her.

"The National Art Honor Society induction. Even though I teach at two schools, we have the induction ceremony at Dulcimer. I'm in charge of fixing the art on each table and I signed up to clean up since the teacher at Dulcimer said she'd set up the refreshments. I shouldn't be too late", she added, wiping her purple nose.

"That's fine. Chase and I are going back out for a while. Taryn, do be careful. We still haven't caught the son of a bitch," I called out to her as she headed for the Pathfinder instead of the Harley. She waved her free arm, and I went into the kitchen to fix a sandwich, watching the sky darken and more rain begin.

I hadn't told Taryn we finally had the search warrant for Haze DeBrew's house. We needed hard evidence. We put a tail on him but the agent was told to keep his distance until we were ready to spring our trap. I just hoped we found what we needed before someone else died.

~~~~~

There was a record turnout for the National Art Society induction. Haze waited in his truck as the rain fell in sheets and the thunder rumbled. He ducked once when lightning struck something near him. He waited until everyone left except Taryn Kosterman, who was in the cafeteria's kitchen. She wrapped leftovers and poured punch back into containers to be frozen for the next event. She turned toward the door when she heard it open. Haze DeBrew entered with his own key and locked the door behind him.

"Why, Haze DeBrew. You scared the living daylights out of me! What're you doing here?"

"I was in the audience. Didn't you see me? My niece paints," he lied. "She thought she left her sweater in here. It's raining so hard I told her I'd run back and get it and drop it by her house later."

Taryn handed him two containers of punch. "I haven't seen a sweater, but, do me a favor and help me get this into the freezer and I'll help you look." She carried the other two containers, and Haze followed her to the Blast chiller, set at minus thirty-two degrees. She went inside and put her containers on the shelf, coming back to get the two he held. Once she turned back toward the shelf again, he slammed the door, thinking this would really piss off Tall Skinny Bitch. He could hear Taryn hollering and beating on the door but he walked to the cafeteria exit, flipped off the lights, and headed for his truck.

Before he reached it, a young black man in a truck drove up. "Who are you and what are you doing on campus?"

The school ID badge around his neck said Coach Lovingood.

Haze didn't like his tone of voice, but showed him his school keys. "I work for the Madison County Schools Maintenance Department. I got a call to check out the alarm system. I didn't realize the banquet was tonight. If people aren't out by ten o'clock, the alarm goes off."

"I don't remember seeing you here before," Evan said. "I teach here."

"I service all the schools. I'm usually here after hours and on weekends. I'm not familiar with you either. Are you new?"

"I came after the semester started. Hey, isn't that Mrs. Kosterman's Pathfinder? Is she in the cafeteria?"

"No, I couldn't find anybody, Coach. She must've ridden somewhere with somebody else. She'll probably come back for it later," Haze theorized, wanting to move the coach farther away from the building. "Hey, since you're here and the rain has stopped, could you do me a favor and help me get the brush chipper on my truck? I have to cut down some bushes in the morning."

Lovingood studied the Pathfinder for a second and walked to the industrial chipper while Haze backed up his truck. The two men lifted the chipper into the bed. Haze thanked him and when the coach turned to leave, hit him in the head with a hammer, stunning him. He pulled the slender man up into the truck bed and shoved his feet down into the chute. He cranked the diesel engine and the coach screamed as his feet and legs were drawn into the feeder wheels, spurting the life out of him.

40

I met Chase at the Sheriff's Department and he displayed the warrant while we gunned out the driveway, heading back up the mountain with reinforcements close behind us. The heavy rain slowed us down but we were determined to find what we needed to arrest DeBrew. When we reached the road into the property, Chase and I drove in while other officers spread out in the woods and one car blocked the way out. Once we got to the house, we knew Haze wasn't there.

"His truck's gone. We're going in," I called over the radio. I could hear a response from the sheriff but Chase and I were already approaching the front door, my blood racing with adrenalin.

"Allow me," Chase said. I backed up and pointed my Ruger at the door. Chase kicked it in and we did a walk-through. When we were satisfied we were alone, we searched for anything that might link Haze to the killings. Chase rummaged through his office desk while I went through the master bedroom.

The smell of urine hit my nose hard. I walked to the unmade bed and saw the stain, remembering I'd learned in a course that many serial killers were bed wetters. I moved to the bathroom door. My eyes came out of their sockets when I saw what was scrawled on the back of it.

"Chase, get in here!" He ran to the bathroom where I stood holding the door. Scrawled on it in blue ink:

A
B
C
D
E
F

"What is this? What does it mean?"

We studied the letters. "Let's see, Roman was suffocated, Paul was beaten, Beech was mutilated," Chase said. I reached over his shoulder with my index finger. "What if suffocated meant asphyxiated? And mutilated meant cut up?" I almost yelled. "I'd be willing to bet it's got something to do with the murders. And, Chase, he's a bed-wetter."

Chase ran toward the kitchen and disappeared into DeBrew's home office. I ran behind him, thinking about the other alphabet letters. Chase plopped into a swivel chair. "Thank God it's on. I thought he'd be smart enough to turn the power off. He must have left in a hurry. I hope he's not on to us." I echoed that feeling.

"Maybe he's storing something on here."

Chase pulled up some files and we both searched for a possible clue. I slammed my index finger on the screen. "Whoa. Click alpha. Let's see what's in that file."

Chase clicked and the screen opened:

A is for asphyxiate, along with a scanned picture of John Roman's obituary;
B is for bury;
C is for cut up, with Joyce Beech's scanned obit;
D is for drown, with the scanned article on Cecilia Nesbitt;
E is for electrocute, with Hank Iroc's obit scanned in;
F was blank.

"My God! Is he going through the alphabet? Chase, we've got to stop him. Cecilia Nesbitt and Hank Iroc weren't accidents at all! He's killed five people! And B. What the hell is this about? Becky Paul was beaten, not buried." I tried to shake off my confusion.

"That bastard beat Becky to a pulp and mutilated that poor black woman," Chase said, half-dazed.

I clutched his arm. "No, Chase. Something's not right. This says buried. Something's wrong about that. But first things first. Where could he be? He could be killing someone else right now. What is F? What the hell is *F*?"

A deputy yelled out from the back porch. We jumped into the doorframe simultaneously and stopped in our tracks at the sight: a frozen right forearm, presumably belonging to Joyce Beech. We told the deputy to get the department's techie to confiscate the computer and to go through its entire contents, and radio for some help to seal off the house and property.

We ran full speed, barely getting wet even though the sky sprung a large leak. I told Chase to drive since he knew his way around better than I did. I called agents and Sheriff Yandle that Haze was our man, but we still had to find him.

"Railey and Hunter, get the hell over to Dulcimer High School. The principal just called. She's hysterical. She says she's at home watching someone die on the school's surveillance camera. She can't make out who it is. We're stuck on a damn log back here in the woods. It's so muddy we can't get out. Get the sonavabitch!" Yandle was gone.

"Chase! Taryn's at Dulcimer tonight! Hurry!"

~~~~~

Chase floored the Hummer's gas pedal and we took the mountain curves at high speed, swishing unsteadily on the wet surface. I was glad he was accustomed to driving these roads, but it didn't keep me from clenching the armrest tight enough to remove all the blood from my knuckles.

Taryn. Was Haze killing her?

We screeched into the dark side of the school near the cafeteria, and Chase floored the Hummer as the headlights engulfed Haze DeBrew, standing in the schoolyard covered in blood. He ran toward his truck. I jumped out and chased him, tackling him before he could get inside and drive off. I threw him to the ground with as much force as I could muster.

I put my nine-millimeter in his face, but he grabbed my arm, making me tumble to the ground beside him. He slapped me hard with the back of his hand and jumped up. So did I, this time planting my feet and aiming the gun's laser through his back. I still had to find Taryn. Otherwise, I would have aimed for his head.

"Freeze! Stop now or die, you bastard!" I yelled at the top of my lungs.

He froze, wearing a sneer. Blood-curdling screams were coming from the chipper. Chase activated a "panic bar" to reverse the feeder wheels so he could rescue Evan Lovingood, the man's limbs now nothing more than ground beef.

The rescue team sped in front of the other agents and Janah Zack.

"Where's Taryn, you bastard? What've you done to her?" I screamed at Haze. He pointed to the cafeteria.

I grabbed the keys from his belt and ran to the kitchen while officers cuffed him. I yelled but got no response.

"Over here! There's nowhere else she could be," yelled Janah, running through the cafeteria's back door to the Blast chiller. Janah fumbled with the keys and got the door open, holding it back so it wouldn't shut again.

I pushed past her to find Taryn in a lump on the floor near the door. We dragged her into the kitchen and I tried to wrap myself around her while Janah screamed for help. Another rescue unit arrived and an EMT ran in with several blankets. I continued to hold Taryn on the floor and bawled.

The EMT checked for a pulse. "Weak, but still alive," she said. A stretcher rolled in and we lifted Taryn onto it.

I walked into the night air. The first unit had left with Evan Lovingood's mangled body. Janah got into her Sequoia to follow. Chase flung Haze DeBrew toward Sheriff Yandle's car and ran to me. We both collapsed on the ground, our emotions taking over. The rescue unit pulled out with Taryn.

"He's gettin' away!" Yandle yelled.

What the hell?

Chase and I jumped up in time to see Haze dive into his truck. He'd backhanded a young deputy to make his break. My long legs stretched full speed as I dove into the slippery truck bed, Chase struggled unsuccessfully to catch up. Haze shimmied the truck down the wet road, trying to throw me out, but I held tight, determined the son of a bitch wouldn't get away from me. Haze drove with cuffs on and too fast for the road conditions. The recent heavy rains coupled with today's rain left the rivers and streams full and the mountainsides muddy and treacherous.

The truck rounded a bend and spun off the road into a swollen creek. We were both in the muddy tempest, trying to survive in frigid water. A piece of someone's deck zipped past with threatening nails sticking up all over it. There was no way to avoid debris if I was in its path. The creek spun us downstream like an undulating conveyor belt. Haze hit a boulder and was stunned long enough for me to grab hold of him. When he threw his cuffed arms up to hit me, I kneed him in the groin, trying to transfer his testicles into his tonsils.

The fast water propelled me on downstream and I braced to go over the side of the mountain when DeBrew's arm appeared from behind me, displaying a busted cuff. He grabbed at me and I dodged his grip, thankful the mud was slippery. I could see Chase on the bank above and I hollered out a warning to him as Haze snatched his leg, bringing him into the water with us.

The three of us plummeted farther downstream in uncontrollable mud, picking up speed. Somehow Haze got past me as I looked for Chase and tried to keep my head above the muck. Haze hit a tree hard, and went over the mountain and out of sight. I tried to grab onto the same tree but it was too slippery and I, too, went over the edge.

I braced for nasty breaks, but landed in a muddy nest of thick kudzu with Chase landing several yards beyond. I pulled my weary body upright and ran to Chase, relieved to see his arm stretch out toward me.

Together we collected an unconscious DeBrew and headed around to a dry area where agents waited for us. We handed the murderer over to them. Chase and I worked our way to the Hummer along the slippery bank, but I lost my footing and quickly slid down into the muddy mess again. I caught debris in the face several times before clutching secured tree branches that snatched me back. I clung with renewed determination and soon heard Chase's yell above me. A rope splashed in front of me and I grabbed it. Chase and two deputies pulled me through the sludge express to an area with no trees and boulders. Chase, now by my side, lifted me to the others. I was spent.

41

Taryn survived. Lovingood didn't. It had taken us over five months to catch Haze DeBrew, who killed at least six innocent people and hurt others on his murderous rampage. The local Sheriff's department wasn't feeling benevolent, and SBI agents moved him to a safer and more secure location to await trial.

After Joyce Beech's arm and Cecilia Nesbitt's watch were presented as evidence, DeBrew admitted to killing everyone but Becky Paul and vowed to get her killer himself. He also said we'd find a body buried some place in the mountains but he couldn't remember where. He said he'd buried some girl up to her head and left her—maybe in the Pisgah Forest—several weeks before. He hallucinated, screamed, and cried about being sexually molested time after time by his father for most of his life. Haze's attorney entered a plea of insanity and a judge ordered him institutionalized for a psychiatric evaluation.

Chase and I joined a search party to comb the hundreds of mountains, following the Appalachian Trail where it cut through Max Patch Mountain in the Pisgah National Forest, thinking that might be a logical place to leave a body, not too far from DeBrew's house.

Without success, we went back to the Sheriff's Department to rest and make a grid of the forest. A call came in that a Janice Yates had gone missing a few weeks before. She was a twenty-one-year-old white female, just hired by Madison County Schools to teach technology courses.

A hunter called a short time later and told us to get to the state line. We sped, confident that Haze DeBrew told the truth this time. We walked through the moist ferns and underbrush, the forest impassable in places. We backtracked to hiking trails or openings, plowing through young foliage that sprung up through thick decay from the past season.

We discovered a clay bank, recently shoveled in one area, the mound of mulch bloody with the stump of a head left, alive with maggots feverishly devouring scraps of flesh.

"Get a shovel!" I yelled. We quickly uncovered the remains of the woman, buried alive and left to be eaten.

"That sonavabitch!" Chase shrieked.

I walked away, brushing my short hair hard enough to remove it. I stood alone for a few minutes until Chase slowly moved beside me. He put his arm around me and I buried my head in his shoulder.

"He's a sick bastard, Logan." Those words weren't malicious enough. I hoped DeBrew roasted in eternal hell.

We walked to the truck and got my PERK. I picked up a few maggots and lifted them into a baggie, hoping their contents would reveal the victim's DNA. Could this be Janice Yates?

42

A gent Hunter?"

"Yes," I said into my cell phone.

The man's throat cleared. "I n..need to t..talk to you." It was DeWayne Lamplighter's stutter.

"What about?"

"I g..got some information."

"About?"

"Meth. C..come to The P..Potato House. Noon. Alone." Dial tone. What was this about? Come alone? And where the hell was The Potato House?

Taryn told me The Potato House was a restaurant near the entrance to the Pisgah Forest, operated by the Cherokee. Chase was tied up with a local investigation, so I figured I might as well find out what Lamplighter wanted. I packed my weapons just in case he had something ugly up his sleeve.

I found The Potato House and went in. I could barely see Lamplighter's big silhouette in the back booth in the dark restaurant. He faced the door so I slid in across from him.

"I knew you'd come. I n..need some help. You're the only one I c..could call."

"What kind of help, DeWayne?"

In a barely audible voice he told me Andrew Railey represented Roy Nesbitt and not him. He said he was afraid they were going to pin everything on him. He was adamant that he only did what Roy told him to. After all, Roy was a deputy.

"I don't see how this has anything…"

"They're in this together. R..Railey's taking care of his boy."

My eyes blinked fast. I tried to comprehend what he told me.

"You g..get it?"

"Are you saying Andrew Railey is involved in the meth?"

"Involved? Hell no! He i..*is* the meth. D..don't you get it? It's his m..money that sets up all the labs in this county. R..Roy watches them because…"

"Because he's a deputy and no one would suspect him."

"Y..yeah."

"DeWayne, do you realize you're saying one of the biggest attorneys in western North Carolina is dirty?"

"I f…figure you're my best chance at j..justice. I'll t..testify in court but you gotta p..protect me. I seen plenty and heard p..plenty. C..can you help me?"

This was a chance to bring down a huge drug operation. Meth is nasty stuff, and its use is an epidemic. I promised him I'd try getting him good representation. This stunning information made me queasy. Chase's dad. Even though they weren't close, how would he take this?

~~~~~

"Chase, I've got some new information. We need to talk about it in private."

"You've got my attention."

I handed him a cheeseburger and took a bite out of mine, chewing and thinking about how to tell him.

"Well?"

"While you were busy, DeWayne Lamplighter called and wanted to talk to me. I went to see him."

He eyed me as if surprised.

"Not smart, but go on."

"He said your father is representing Roy Nesbitt."

"I'm not surprised."

"DeWayne was upset because your dad represents Roy but not him. He thinks he's going to be fingered for the marijuana and the meth."

"And he can probably get Roy off like hundreds before him."

"He said something else interesting, hoping I'd try to get him decent representation."

"It would have to be mighty good information along with some proof."

"If he's telling the truth, Chase, it's excellent information that could bring down the drug operation in Madison County."

He gave me his full attention. "Out with it! What's this important information?"

I told him DeWayne knew who was behind the meth labs.

"For Pete's sake, Logan, do I have to pull it out of you?"

"Andrew Railey," I blurted.

He stared for a second and ran his fingers through his blond waves. He stood and walked across the room. I waited.

"Is he sure? Does he have proof?"

"I'm not sure if he has anything we can really use, but he swears on his life your father is the money behind all of it."

"Shit! I'm not that surprised, really." I remained quiet. What could I say? His dad's a real jerk, but a criminal? That was going to be hard for Chase to swallow. He turned to me. "We're going to nail his ass, Logan. He needs to be in jail right beside all the low lifes he's gotten off time after time," he said with conviction. Chase grabbed my arm. "Let's go."

I had no idea where we were going but I stood. I hoped it wasn't to confront his father. When we got to Asheville, Chase drove into the posh Dill Hill gated community, showing his badge to get past the security guard. We circled several blocks twice and went on down the street until he stopped at a paved driveway in front of a brown brick house. We knocked on the door and a beautiful blonde seemed surprised to see us.

I showed her my badge and she invited us in. "The SBI? I don't understand. What can I do for you?" She glanced at Chase and apparently realized she should know him. "Aren't you..."

"Chase Railey, yes. You're my father's mistress."

The blonde's knees and mine both buckled. She hurried to a door and closed it. "What's this about? Why are you here? Has something happened to Drew?"

"Not yet."

"What do you mean? Is he all right?"

I stayed quiet and let Chase do what he'd come to do. "Is your husband home?"

"No. Why? Has Bruce done something wrong?"

"Let me tell you why we're here, Marilyn. You don't mind if I call you Marilyn, do you?" Chase's voice was harsh.

"You're sleeping with my dad. You have been for several years, right?" Before she could respond, he continued. "Agent Hunter and I are working on a case and we need your help. I'm sure you'll be glad to help us, won't you, Marilyn?"

"I don't know. I mean, I...your dad and I—"

"Enough small talk, Marilyn. I'm sure he talks to you about his work and investments, right?"

"You need to leave. I don't want you here anymore."

"We're not leaving. We'll wait until your husband gets home so he can hear the conversation. Bet he'd be real interested."

Her face blanched. "What do you want?" Her voice was shaky and her hands began to twitch.

"I want you to testify against my father. You know, about his meth labs and all the other drug deals he's got going on."

"I can't do that! He'd kill me!"

"So you do know about his illegal operations." It was a statement, not a question.

"I can't help you," she said adamantly.

"Fine. Agent Hunter and I will make ourselves comfortable until your husband arrives." Chase settled into a chair.

"No, please! Can't we work something out? I promise not to see him anymore. That's what you really want, isn't it? I'll do that. I'll call him right now and tell him it's over." She walked quickly to the phone but Chase moved quicker, took it out of her hands, and replaced it in the cradle.

"Nice try, but I'm not buying." Chase was in her face, speaking quietly and calmly.

The blonde dissolved into tears. I turned on my mini recorder as Chase pulled information from her. She didn't know where the labs were located but she knew they existed. He'd told her on more than one occasion the jewelry he gave her came from meth money.

Chase promised her protection for her cooperation, and told her if she made contact with Andrew Railey, her husband would be expeditiously informed of the affair and she would be charged as an accessory.

~~~~~

We sat down with Sheriff Yandle. He recommended a lawyer for Lamplighter and we made a plan to get Mr. Railey. Although we convinced Marilyn to help us, we wired DeWayne, somewhat worried about his clumsiness, but we needed more evidence.

Dewayne demanded a meeting with Railey in a place we could easily survey. DeWayne told him he was going to squeal if he didn't meet him. Railey agreed to show up. A nervous Lamplighter walked out to meet the black Mercedes when it approached. I whispered to him to stay back until Railey got out; I was afraid the attorney might have a gun. DeWayne pulled back and waited. Railey threw open the door and stepped out.

"What's this about, Lamplighter? What are you trying to pull?"

"I j..just want what's f..fair, that's all."

"Fair?" Railey threw back his head and laughed. "Nothing is fair, Cherokee. You ought to know that."

"If you g..get Roy off, you can get me off too. We're all in this together, Roy, me and…you."

"Are you threatening me? I don't take kindly to threats. You need to listen. I've got it all planned. You won't have to do much time. I'll help you by making a deal with your lawyer."

"No. Not if R..Roy gets off. It ain't fair for me to do time."

Railey walked closer to DeWayne. I was pleased that every word came in loud and clear. "I'll make it worth your while to take the wrap, Cherokee."

"M..my name's DeWayne."

"Well, DE Wayne, as soon as you're out, I'll give you your own meth lab. You'll be in charge, run the whole set up like you want to instead of breaking and entering to steal. There's plenty to go around, Cherokee. Meth's the biggest drug now. I'll tell you what, I'll even give you a lab on wheels, you know, an RV lab."

The sheriff had heard enough. The Madison County squad jumped into action as Andrew Railey realized too late he'd been set up. His car was surrounded and they waited for Chase to make his move. He walked over to his father.

"Chase, what is this?" He attempted a pitiful laugh.

Chase grabbed him and spun him around to the car, slamming him hard on the hood. "Andrew Railey, you're under arrest. Anything you say can and will be used against you in a court of law." The words were sullen and matter-of-fact, as though this were just another arrest.

43

Word soon came of Haze's demise. He'd become arrogant about all the killings and got himself raped and tortured in jail by a huge inmate. When he tried to retaliate, the inmates in the yard beat him to death. My words froze in the air as I said them.

"He had it coming."

We could begin to relax a little now and Trust could begin to heal. We decided to celebrate with dinner at the newest bistro in Asheville. Dinner was delicious but we were quiet, even though the place overflowed with rowdy people. We were exhausted. Months of investigating, interviewing, and chasing had taken its toll on both of us. Nevertheless, something bothered me and I sensed that the same thing worried Chase.

"Chase, one of the guards said Haze swore repeatedly he didn't kill Becky. What if he told the truth? He admitted to everything else, even the ones we thought were accidents." He glared at me. "I mean, just what if?"

"Are you saying what I think you're saying?"

"I think there's another killer."

~~~~~

We headed west to talk to our best suspect, whom we'd heard was possibly molested by his stepfather as a child. But the mountains seemed too full of molestation and incest stories. They couldn't all be true.

When we pulled in the drive, Steve Paul and his little girls, Bea and Ally, were on the front porch. We got out and walked up as he put an arm around each girl.

"How are things going, Steve?"

"Okay, I guess," he replied in a strangely soft and sad voice, still holding on to the girls who were motionless.

"Hello, Bea. Hi, Ally." They looked at us, but said nothing.

"I know it's tough for all of you," Chase began.

"Tough don't begin to describe it."

"What can we do to help?"

Steve fixed his eyes on me. "There's nothing anybody can do. It's all over."

"Steve, why not let the girls go for a ride in Logan's Hummer and I'll sit with you on the porch for a while?"

His grip tightened on the girls. "No! They stay with me." He shifted a little. "I need to get them inside for some dinner. Come back later," he said, managing a crooked smile.

Chase and I backed off the porch a few steps as Steve motioned the girls into the house. We both knew something was wrong. The girls weren't acting right, but then they had recently lost their mother in a violent way.

Steve went inside, pushing them in front of him. I positioned my fingers on my gun, still hoping we were wrong. We went around the side of the large house, then heard a truck door slam and ran back toward the front.

Steve came by us, slinging his dualie all over the yard, barely missing the Hummer. He waved a .357 Magnum to warn us. The girls, against their will, were in for the ride of their young lives. We ran for the Hummer and went after them.

"I guess that answers the question. I just can't believe Steve could kill Becky." We rounded sharp curves, heading down the mountain toward Pig Meadow too fast.

"If he gets to the Possum Creek Tomato Cannery we may never find him. That place is huge. I see his taillights. Hurry, Logan. He can duck in too many places. He knows these mountains better than most. Hurry up!"

I wanted to give Chase a fierce look, but I couldn't afford to take my eyes off the road even for a second. The switchbacks got tougher as we went down and around. I could barely make out the lights ahead, losing ground with every twist in the road. My knuckles were white and my fingers dug into the steering wheel while my intestines tied themselves into knots.

"Move, Logan, move!" yelled an excited Chase.

"Shut the hell up, Chase! Don't say another fricking word or I'll dump you out right here!" That did it. Silence.

I maneuvered the Hummer, keeping the truck in sight. Up. Down. Around. Switching back. I navigated two more curves and couldn't see anything down The Flats, a three-mile strip of straight, flat road ahead.

"Damn! Where'd we lose him?" I slowed from ninety to eighty, about to take a breath of air for the first time in twelve miles, when the dualie sprang into the road behind me, coming hard.

"Shit!" Chase pulled his gun back out. I waved my arm.

"No, Chase, the girls!" I got my hand back on the wheel before the dualie bumped us on the next down slope. I hung on to the wheel and managed to keep the Hummer under control. He came at us again in a curve and I white-knuckled around the mountain's edge, spitting rocks. Too close. No time to let up. I floored the Hummer as the road straightened ahead of us and left Steve some distance behind. I pulled over to wait for him to catch up so I could return the intimidation.

Chase and I both panted as we waited. And waited. And waited. "Where the hell is he?"

Chase straightened up and squirreled his neck down the road. "Maybe we missed a road. We should head back. They could have wrecked and the girls might need us."

I pulled out and headed back. After about two miles back Chase pointed off to the left. The sign read Plum Cove.

"Take it. I bet he went this way. There's an old gem mine back in there."

Sure enough, Steve's truck was parked, but he and the girls were gone. Nearby were two backhoes and a track hoe to move dirt. Chase and I entered the mouth of a wild cave with guns drawn. We moved slowly, listening for any indication of where they were. I listened intently, my ears perked all I could perk them but the wood frogs just outside were so earsplitting I couldn't hear a damn thing over them.

Chase motioned to me, indicating he heard something in front of us in the dark. We moved cautiously down each side of the cave, having to let our eyes adjust to the darkness. I pulled out my penlight to guide us. I caught stalagmites in its beam. I heard one of the girls whimper off to my left. We moved slowly toward another dark hole where just enough light came from God knows where to throw a shadow on the cave wall, high up. We braced for an ambush as we both jumped around the juts in the cave, only to see Steve running into a light at the other end, a girl under each arm.

Chase and I scampered into the brightness, at first blinded. I heard a noise and turned to see one of the girls sliding down a panning flume. I raced to her and she jumped into my arms, screaming hysterically. I took the older girl to the Hummer and told her to lock herself in.

"Don't open the doors until I come back. Don't get out for any reason."

"Daddy's got Bea. And a gun."

"Stay put."

I ran in the direction Chase went and about the time I reached him we heard the backhoe coming. Steve barreled toward us, steering with one hand, clutching Bea to his chest with the other. I couldn't get a clear shot at him. He was manic. We leapt out of the backhoe's path. After several attempts to crush us, he lost control and got the bucket of the backhoe stuck in a cave entrance. We raced at him with guns, but he dragged a kicking and screaming Bea with him into another cave.

"Logan," Chase whispered, "I'm going to try to talk to him. You find another way in."

Fortunately I was thin enough to lie on my back and crawl backwards through a small opening near the cave entrance. I felt a twinge of claustrophobia before I reached the other side, twisting and contorting my body, hoping I wasn't burying myself in an airless tomb. I could hear water when I quietly stood in the darkness on the other side. I aimed my light slowly and gasped at the magnificent underground waterfall caught in its beam. Off in the distance I could hear a loud conversation. I eased toward it cautiously, trying to stay out of Steve's vision.

"Steve? It's Chase, man. I just want to have a word with you."

"Go away! Get the hell out of here!" The voice was shrill, unrecognizable. I could hear Bea sobbing. Chase walked with his fingers touching his holster. Steve Paul, holding the .357, was between Chase and me, with Bea close to him. "Don't come any closer, Chase. I'll kill her."

Chase put his hands in the air. "Steve, I just want to talk. Let her go. I'm on your side, man."

Steve snarled. "Yeah, right. Where's your partner? Tell her to get around here where I can see her. I ain't playin' now!" He smashed the gun into Bea's temple.

"She's coming. She's just a little claustrophobic, doesn't like dark tight places. She's behind me. Don't do anything stupid, man. I know you don't really want to hurt her," nodding at Bea.

Steve Paul began to weep but he wasn't letting go of his younger daughter.

"Why, Steve? What happened?"

"Becky ran out on me. She was seeing Haze. She aimed to leave us," Steve blubbered out.

"What? No, no, Steve. You got it all wrong. Haze was harassing *her*. She reported him to her principal and even went to a psychiatrist about him. She loved you and wanted Haze to leave her alone. I'm for real, man. I know you don't want to hurt Bea."

Using the girl's name made Steve glance down. "Why didn't she tell me? I could've taken care of that sonavabitch. I should've done something a long time ago. Now I've ruined our lives. There's no reason for us to live. Once you lock me up, there's nobody for the girls. They'll be better off dead." He pulled Bea closer and put the gun to her temple.

The shot penetrated, and Bea ran screaming to Chase as Steve fell forward, my shot striking him above the right eye. Chase gathered the hysterical child in his arms while I tried to grab Steve. I missed. He crumbled in a heap at the bottom of the waterfall at least seventy-five yards below. Motionless.

44

After a late night of paperwork, I sat in Taryn's sunroom. Once again, I sensed him. I walked out to the path and stood motionless. He moved through the fog, one hesitant paw at a time, until we were face to face, neither of us afraid. We made eye contact and held our gaze as I slowly moved my fist toward him. He took another step and pushed his snout out to sniff. I didn't flinch as he licked my fist, then my trusting fingers. He walked slowly away from me, looking back over his shoulder only once. I took this encounter as a good omen.

I breathed a sigh of relief, surprisingly calm, and satisfied the good people of Trust could now regain their resoluteness. At last they could begin the arduous task of healing in this beautiful piece of Earth.

NEXT IN THE LOGAN HUNTER SERIES
HELL SWAMP

Agent Logan Hunter's cast iron stomach and steeled nerves are put to the test in Hell Swamp, a place where snakes, skulls, and sinister secrets abound.

Called back into action from her personal leave to track down a sadistic murderer, Logan traveled to a location in the backwoods of North Carolina, not far from where she grew up.

Across Beatty's Bridge, the familiar Greek revival mansion along the Black River now held a crime scene beyond anyone's worst nightmare. A gruesome mess with blood tracked everywhere, and key evidence already obliterated. With the SBI seriously shorthanded Agent Hunter had the daunting task of piecing everything together to find the killer.

She questioned a strange assortment of suspects and soon discovered the seemingly harmless victim had numerous enemies. Which one committed the heinous crime?

Inching closer to the truth, she dodged increasing danger around every curve as the killer tried to stop her investigation. Even more troubling than the physical attacks, this case brought back Logan's night terrors as she battled Hell Swamp's demons from the past.

After Hell Swamp, the Logan Hunter Series will
continue with
Sin Creek

The Cape Fear River snakes through eastern North Carolina past the stunning port city of Wilmington and sidles up next to Gator Creek, a sliver of water where wickedness and decadence take precedence over decency.

About Author Susan Whitfield

Award-winning multi-genre author Susan Whitfield is a native of North Carolina, where she sets all of her novels. She is the author of five published mysteries, *Genesis Beach*, *Just North of Luck*, *Hell Swamp*, *Sin Creek* and *Sticking Point*. She also authored *Killer Recipes*, a unique cookbook that includes recipes from mystery writers around the country. *Slightly Cracked* is her first women's fiction, set in Wayne County where she lives with her husband. Their two sons live nearby with their families.

Susan's a member of Mystery Writers of America, Sisters in Crime, Coastal Carolina Mystery Writers, and North Carolina Writers Network. Her books are available in print and ebook formats. Susan is currently researching a medieval ancestor for an historical mystery. Learn more at www.susanwhitfieldonline.com

www.ingramcontent.com/pod-product-compliance
Lightning Source LLC
Chambersburg PA
CBHW030145180626
46812CB00002B/857